THE UNDERTOW
BY
CHRISTY L. BONSTELL

Dedicated to: my mother, my son and the Great Lakes.

CHAPTER 1

It's not supposed to be like this. You're not supposed to know. You're not supposed to be aware. It's supposed to be like anesthesia—one minute you're there, the next, you're not. But sometimes, and I know this now, something goes wrong. And the anesthesia drifts through your body, and your body sleeps. But your mind, your mind stays afloat, crashing on the inside of your skull. You open your mouth to scream, but the scream stays put, trapped in the realm of thought, unable to escape your lips, unable to convince your voice to play along.

I don't remember being born the first time, but I remember dying.

In the times since, each birth is clear, but not new; like something you did easily as a child becoming clumsy in your adult hands.

I don't know why I can remember. I get the sense that something is broken, that I'm a lost piece of data no one can see in the sea of information that is our souls. There's no one to ask. No one to explain it to me. And so, I drift though life, or lives rather, awake and aware, no matter how many times I die. No matter how much I am reborn.

I know I am supposed to learn something, but no one has told me this and even if they did— life gets in the way of learning. What I have learned is that time is not what I assumed time to be. It doesn't go forward or backward. It's not a loop. It's all the time. All of the time is happening all of the time, but you are only in one place at a time. Right now I am here, but tomorrow I could be born yesterday. A soul does not belong to just one person, but to everything surrounding it. You can be in two places at once because time has more than one dimension and there's more to any of us than skin and bones and brain. We are powerful, all things, made of dust and light and that dust and light belongs to everything. Humans assign these words to define time, but time isn't for us to wrangle, refusing to be shoved into a neatly marked file folder. Time just is. So I don't go after or before, only to a different time than where I currently am.

But I stay here. I am always here. It turns out, at least for me, though time may change, my soul lives here. Always in the same place. No matter what I am born, I am always here, with the dark waters of Lake Michigan in reach, with sand dune residue on my skin. Once I figured out what was happening I'd desperately wished that I might see Egypt or Japan. Fly across oceans, smell volcano ash, see how some man-made mystery was accomplished. But I do not. I am home. And, after a while, this is a comfort to me. No matter who (or what) I am; I am here.

As I said, I don't remember my first birth, but I'm told it was unremarkable in every way, aside from being a week early and catching my mother slightly off-guard as she made potato-salad for the church picnic. We lived in a fine house on the top of a dune, over-looking the lake.

My room was grey-blue and faced the water and at times, if I squinted, I felt like I could disappear into the mass of sea and sky and stay there forever.

I do not remember my name. Nor do I remember having any particular attachment to it or particularly disliking it. It's funny how some things stay with you when you review your life and yet things we place such a premium on, like names, are so utterly irrelevant. Naming a person is like naming a breeze; it's gone before you can utter it. Naming is more for the namer than the named.

I struggled with her name. Maybe I sensed somehow that to name is to attach oneself and attaching yourself to another person is an exercise in futility. You can't even attach yourself to a body. Not that I knew that then, exactly, but maybe I sensed it.

I don't remember wanting to be pregnant. It was spring, 1960 and the leaves were just resetting themselves on the trees, turning the clouded and inhospitable lakeside into a fairytale. I was married, I remember, but I don't remember his face. Like much of that life, everything had the sense that I was just off the mark. That I was just right off the bull's-eye. I shrugged a lot. I thought little. I examined nothing. I was happy in the way that the lake is happy—placid and cool, so plain it seems fake.

I've heard women say, both then and in lives since, that they'd never felt more lovely than when they were pregnant. Often they'd add that they felt more feminine, more connected to the holy, more important somehow. I did not share this feeling. Being pregnant seemed to make each and every task more oppressive than the last. My fingers swelled in time with my stomach. And, while I did not suffer morning sickness, I was constantly uncomfortable. Like wearing a too large suit of armor—everything was heavy and rubbed the wrong areas.

I tried to keep up with my social duties. I didn't work, but I volunteered with a dune restoration project and dedicated myself to it fully. In the early part of the 1900s, the dunes surrounding Lake Michigan were leveled, left barren and bald, to feed the great mouth of Chicago. One by one the timbers fell, floated across the lake and arrived to build skyscrapers and railroads and otherwise keep industry moving the only direction it heads—blindly forward. What once had been great and deep forests, became empty mounds of the finest golden sand you've ever seen. The dunes were lovely, and if you squinted your eyes and thought fantastical thoughts, you could almost imagine you were in some far off land like Saudi Arabia. Many times as a young girl, feet planted in those dunes, head held high, I'd imagine just such things.

But without roots, the dunes threatened to blow away. To cover the lake. To disappear.

Like I said, it was the 60s and people were turning back to the earth, offering apologies for the damage done, doing their best to make amends. And so, an effort was made to restore the forest to the dunes. But how does one go about planting roots in a medium that won't stop shifting? Every time you'd kneel down to plant a wind would blow and the thing you were just looking at would be rearranged. It was slow work. But little by little dune grasses were planted by hundreds of volunteers. Once the roots were set, the hope was the dunes would stop their slow walk to the sea.

So I volunteered twice a week in this effort. At first I was just more tired than usual and the already arduous task of climbing a dune became even more difficult. Each step made me want to lay down in the warm sand, let it conform to my body, feel the cool, wet packed sand underneath as I sank and slept. As my belly grew rounder, bending over became nearly impossible and I'd spend long stretches crawling on my hands and knees planting row after row of sharp grass.

It wasn't that I couldn't have worked. I could have. My husband had no quarrel with women working outside of the home and I had gone to school to become a bookkeeper. I liked the way the numbers lined up into neat patterns and rearranged themselves to make more patterns, like a never-ending kaleidoscope of digits. It's likely the same part of me that enjoyed watching the neat rows of grasses go in, little by little, multiplying daily. But I was pregnant within a month of our wedding night and so it seemed rather useless to find a job when I'd just have to quit in nine months.

My parents had passed away when I was 16 and the little dune house had been left to me. It was March and they were driving my father's new car, a fine piece of Detroit steel, and a storm hit Lakeshore Drive suddenly. Storms come off of the lake with such force that one minute you can be gardening in short sleeves and 10 minutes later be under a thick blanket of wet and heavy snow. They had been in Saugatuck, a charming boat town just north, celebrating their anniversary. Their car went careening off the road and into the lake, which was still partially frozen from a beastly winter.

They died holding hands. Some things you remember no matter how many lives you live.

The little house on the dune had been all mine and my husband and I saw no need to buy another.

Week after week I'd return to my volunteering and as my child grew, the dune began to change shape. Sometimes, when the sun was high, I'd see my shadow on the face of the dune, the roundness of my stomach inside the roundness of the tan mass of sand. It looked like the dune was pregnant with me. Like a nesting doll of pregnant things.

By November a chill moved in and the growth was measurable both in the dunes and in myself. My child moved inside of me with a force that seemed, at times, aggressive. Like I was keeping the baby hostage and it wanted nothing more than to be released from the prison of my body. I hated the amount of sitting and resting and sleeping that needed to be done. I too, felt captive by my body and I was calmed knowing at least the baby and I had that in common.

Outside, the earth changed daily. The sun seemed watered down and I saw less of it, both because of the planet's ceaseless journey and the lack of hours I was awake. The lake turned angry and threw itself at the shore. It fought its inevitable immobility. Soon it would be frozen in time, and despite knowing it would be born again in the spring, it could not help but rage against its impending icy state. I stared at it for hours as it rose and fell, turned from glass to froth. On grey days you couldn't tell where the horizon began and ended and I wondered the same of myself. Did I end where the child began? Or were we in this together, a yin and yang of bodies.

The snow started gently as the winter set in, dusting the few trees left on the dunes and the dunes themselves. Outside the air was wet and heavy as the lake welcomed back the water that escaped to the heavens in the dry heat of August. I was tired, but then, so was the beach, which seemed to pull a blanket over its tanned shoulders and prepare to sleep. I stood outside, willing the air to wake me up. I was ready for this to be over.

I'd spent the last of my energy readying my childhood room to be a nursery. I swept the floors and retrieved my bassinet from the attic. I left the walls the same—hoping the child would feel as I had—wrapped into the world of the sea and the sky.

In the summer, one of the volunteers, noticing my larger-than-average protrusion, good-naturedly told me I'd need a teaspoon full of castor oil to kick the birth off early before I turned into a solid ball of flesh. I'd laughed then, but it was easy to laugh then. The sun had shone on my face, warming my already increasingly warm flesh. My hands had been in the earth. The future seemed far away.

But now the sun was gone. The warmth I'd felt had turned into an aching heat in each of my joints and I sweat despite being freezing. The baby wasn't due for another two weeks, but I prayed daily that the end was near. My husband had taken to calling me "little duck" because of the way I waddled thought the house, like a drunken bird pretending to be sober.

I thought on the castor oil.

The body has a funny way of preparing you for motherhood. In the final stretch, which somehow seems longer than the previous eight months combined, the torture compounds itself by also not allowing you sleep. You're tired constantly, but sleep evades you in the same way the waves pull back from the shore. It's meant to train you. To toughen you up. To help you learn, before taking care of a tiny life, how to operate while nearly sleepless without killing yourself or others.

So yes, I was done. I'd been to the doctor a week before and he'd said I'd go into labor any day. That had been seven days ago and still I was as round as the moon. I padded into the bathroom. When I was a little girl my mother had given me a tablespoon of castor oil to help ease a tummy ache. It had worked within moments. My system relaxed and my stomachache disappeared. Maybe this would be the same.

I twisted open the cap, poured a capful and drank it. I'd forgotten how terrible the taste was. How slick and viscous my throat felt. No amount of water could wash it away.

I waited. I continued to wait, right there in the bathroom for much of the afternoon. When it appeared nothing was going to happen, I got up and went about the task of preparing dinner. I felt nothing, save for a lingering disappointment in my continued pregnancy.

That night I dreamt I approached the lake at night, the moon floating on her surface, her placid body mirroring the dark sky. I was thirsty. I was more thirsty, in fact, than I could remember having ever been. My mouth was dry, my lips cracked and painful. I bent down and drank. Once I started I could not stop. And I drank and I drank until I drained the lake, leaving its sandy bottom bare. I filled up, my belly swollen, until I felt I would burst. But I could not stop drinking, almost as though it were a habit I'd developed and continued in, passed the point of enjoyment, out of a combination of stubbornness and familiarity. I felt the seams of my body stretch—pushing and straining and I was amazed and proud at how adaptable I was. I regretted, suddenly, never having pushed myself this far prior to this moment. I had, simply, existed without questioning what the limits of my existence were. I continued to expand. Until I felt a slight tear and then another one. Like a ship that sustains a small damage, but that break in the overall structure causes a rippling effect and soon the hull is shot to pieces. And before I know it, I am giving the water back to the sea, or it is taking itself back. I can longer tell which of us is in control.

I bolt upright in a cold sweat, marveling at how damp the sheets are and wondering if I'm stuck in that grey place between dream and reality. But the edges are not soft and the pain I feel is very sharp and I realize that I am, in fact, bursting at the seams. My water has broken, drowning the bed. I do not have time to feel embarrassed. Instead, another undulating wave of pain crashes over me and I am sucked underneath the undertow, unable to breathe as my chest is crushed and I fight for breath. I remember, suddenly, that I did not drink the sea. I wake my husband in between contractions and we pile into the car, with the small bag I've packed, which now seems so silly and trivial.

There was no pain. As had been explained to me by the young physician that would be delivering my child, I arrived at the hospital, was administered drugs, and moments later I was barely able to keep my consciousness. The whole experience was like swimming in water where the temperature is so close to your skin that you can't tell where you begin and the water ends.

I heard the scuffle around me. Saw flashes of lights and shiny metal. I remember wondering if I should be so relaxed at a time like this, and comforted myself with the thought that surely a doctor knew better than I. My husband had removed himself to the expectant father waiting area. I suppose I should have been angry with that, but I also felt like I was so far removed from what was occurring I couldn't find it in me to be the least bit upset.

Time is a funny thing, particularly when you've died and been reborn more times than you can count. Once you realize that time is not bound to rules, it doesn't just move in a way that makes sense to you, you can see how little is up to us and how much of it is truly happenstance. You only make things harder when you lay hands on time, try to name and manipulate it, try and control it. That's where you get into trouble.

The time passed so slowly I felt I could have birthed a hundred babies in that time. In reality it was several hours. But with no pain markers to hold on to, no memories to look back on, it was like standing in the middle of a dessert and trying to ascertain how far I was from where I started. A young nurse pursed her lips together and stood over me, her dark brown hair carefully tucked up into her nurse's cap.

I thought, how nice it must be to be surrounded by educated people. To go to work each day and be a person who did things. To have handsome doctors tell you to fetch this thing or that thing. To have a uniform that identified you as something. Maybe, after the baby was older, I'd be a nurse, too.

The nurse looked concerned. Maybe this was her first birth, I thought. After all, everyone must have a first baby they deliver. And unlike the first cake you bake or a first kiss—this is a first that must be perfect. No learning curve allowed. She looked at me and said, "The baby is nearly here."

About time. This baby had taken months to get here and even longer to leave. I thought about the nap that had been calling me for hours that I'd soon be able to give into.

I felt a tear. Not physically, but in the fabric of my surroundings. Like the room and the walls opened slightly, lost their permanency. I swore I could see clear to the other side of the hospital, where my husband was removing a cold can of soda from a vending machine. His hands were shaking.

It got very loud in just a few moments. There were beeps and voices that were unnaturally high and heavy and seemed to be trying to escape the confines of the body they were in. Soon that faded away, or maybe it was still there but had been overcome. I found myself wondering how I had ended up in the lake. The roar of the waves were inside my head and I could feel nothing else. I started to close my eyes. To relax in a sound so familiar, so soothing. A nurse shook me. She had tears in her eyes. She put a baby in arms. I wanted to tell her that wasn't safe because babies can't swim but my breath was no longer in my throat.

Her face.

Her face, so perfect and calm. I thought, how lucky am I to have given birth to a baby that can be under water and yet so calm. Her hair was the color of sand. Her skin the color of a breaking wave. And she opened her eyes and I saw myself reflected back to me in a shallow puddle of perfect blue water. And just as the love I hadn't known was there began to swell inside of me, I felt the water take me away. The lake wrapped its arms around me and pulled me to the bottom. I tried to fight my way back to the surface, but my body was too heavy to float. As I sank I saw her eyes consider me, love me, need me—will me to live in a way I never had.

But it was all too late and I was gone.

CHAPTER 2

Gone.

What an interesting word. Nothing is ever really gone, I know that now. You're gone from the place where that time and location collide, but never really gone.

There is a light when you leave. And you do float towards it. For most people the story ends there. I expected the same for myself and so I fought. I tried to reach back down and pull myself towards my body—towards the daughter I now wanted so badly to live my life with.

I never even learned her name. I'd searched, while pregnant, through book after book for her name. A boy's name had been chosen (my husband's name) but the girl's names eluded me. I searched through baby-naming books. Through my favorite novels. I listened on the radio and on the television for a series of sounds that would call to the being in my belly, but nothing did. Old women stopped me on the street to offer their opinions; most often their own name. So, when the time had come, I still hadn't named her. I suppose in some way I was hoping she'd name herself upon arriving.

No matter how hard I fought to drive myself back towards the earth, I made no headway. I fought until I was too exhausted to fight anymore. Then I closed my eyes and slept.

CHAPTER 3

I am waking up. I feel as though I've slumbered a thousand years and my arms and legs feel both atrophied and yet lighter somehow, as though they are my legs, yet not my legs. I stretch myself wide. I'm under some sort of covering and I've not yet opened my eyes. When I do I am shocked to find I am nearly blind and all I see in front of me is a grey sheet of some opaque material. I know, instinctively, I must push through it.

I do. And as I do the warmth of the sun hits my back and I am happy. I stretch again, taking in the moist air around me. But this time, when I stretch, there is more to me than there had been and suddenly I am floating in the air, the ground below me looking terrifyingly huge. I recognize the smell (my ability to smell is greatly improved) as the forests surrounding Lake Michigan. I cannot tell if they are larger or I am smaller, but I find comfort in my familiar surroundings.

The sound is unbearably loud. Like a jet plane landing on a runway in my head. I am not alone. In fact, there are thousands around me. My brothers and sisters, born with me here and now a family of many.

I am a mosquito.

My first thought, each time I am born, is of my daughter. I have no clue if each new life will be my last life, but I am desperate to find a way back to her. To see myself, no matter what myself may be, reflected in those clear blue eyes one more time.

But the life of the thing I am takes over and my knowledge that I have been reborn starts to fade. I want to think more on my situation, but right now, I am too hungry to think. I am hungry in a way I have never been hungry. I am so hungry that it consumes my brain, replacing all other thoughts. And I am only hungry for one thing.

The minute I think the word I smell it. I smell different types of blood the way a sommelier might smell wine. Some of it, I identify quickly as dead. It's acrid stench upsetting and confusing my system.

But live blood I find I cannot only smell, but feel, pulsing through my tiny body. I hone in on it and even though I can't see the way I could when I was human, the smell is so thick and clear it's as though I can see it. And there are options, I realize. Different bouquets from different animals, some sweet, some hearty and rich. I fly to the nearest scent, but a light breeze sifts through the air and my little wings are virtually useless against it. Before I can land, my meal has moved. There are other choices. Just as I start to land on a decent second choice, I smell something undeniable. I don't quite know what it is, I cannot place it. But I adjust my flight pattern and float towards it.

I'm excited. To eat? Yes. Something inside of me tells me there is an invisible timer on my life that is directly linked to a blood meal. But it's more than that. And if I could just clear my head of this body's insatiable need to drink, I could think on it.

But I'm torn between a brain of another body and the organism that currently houses it and so I just give in.

I'm close now and surprised by how exhausted the trip has made me. I was born today and I suppose being born takes up an awful lot of energy, but still, this tiny body seems ill designed. I alight on my prey, too tired to think much on what I'm doing. I drink until I am full. It takes only a second, but I can feel myself swell, like a balloon filled with jelly. It's all automatic and for a brief moment I wonder at that. How capable one organism can be, at birth, and how utterly unprepared others are.

My needs met, I withdraw my feeding mechanism and realize where I am. Just as soon as the thought strikes my brain, I am taken, once again from the earth.

CHAPTER 4

I know I shouldn't have let it bite me, but I wanted to see how it worked.

My dad says "being six sure is hard." But he says it in that way that means he doesn't think that at all. I don't like when adults talk like that. I wish they'd just say what they mean.

But it is hard being six because you make a lot of mistakes. Some days it feels like all I do is wake up, make mistakes all day and then go to bed. I don't mean to make mistakes, but I never know something is a mistake until someone else tells me, so how could I stop myself before I do it? That's the hard part about being six. Waiting on everyone else to tell you what's a mistake when they really should just tell you all the rules, right at the beginning.

This summer has been full of mistakes. It's August now and I'll go into the first grade in a couple weeks. My dad calls these "the dog days of summer," but I haven't seen a single dog. I wish adults would just say what they mean.

My dad works at home, so I don't go to camps like my friend Josie. He says it's nice to be with me, but I'd rather be swimming in a pool or running an obstacle course or riding horses or whatever my friends are doing at camp. But I don't want to hurt his feelings because he seems sad and tired a lot and I make a lot of mistakes and that doesn't help.

The summer started with a big mistake. The day I got out of school I wanted to learn to ride a bike so I could visit my friends down the street. My dad said I'd have to wait until we could go into town and buy me a proper little kids bike with training wheels and streamers and stuff. Then he went upstairs to finish working. I went out to the garage, looking for my ball, and that's when I saw it. I didn't know it was hers. I didn't know it was special.

It was bright green, the color of the leaves right after it rains in May. It had shiny handlebars and a long leather seat that looked very adult. But still, I thought, I can ride it. I figured I'd just peddle around until I got the hang of it and then dad would see I didn't need any stupid training wheels.

I rolled it out of the garage and onto the driveway. It looked smaller next to the car and in the dark garage shadows. Now, out in the light, metal gleaming, it's a lot bigger than I am. But a lot of things are bigger than I am and so far it's been ok.

So I throw my leg over the center and try and put my butt on the seat, but it's too tall and I can't seem to get there. After a few minutes of trying, I can perch there just a little, and I start trying to get the pedals to work. I'd had a tricycle when I was a baby, so I get the idea, but my feet just won't cooperate. I'm hungry and I want a snack and I think about bringing the bike back in, but something inside of me says that if I keep trying, I'll get it. Dad always says "just keep trying" when I'm learning my numbers. I hate numbers. Whenever I think I'm getting it, they flip themselves around and become something else entirely.

So I keep trying. And for just a second I'm doing it and it feels like flying. And I'm so proud and happy and free, that I don't see the car coming down the road. I never even notice it hits me.

When I woke up, dad was sitting next to me. We're in the hospital, which I recognize because I came to see Nana here before she went to live in the sky. Dad is sitting in a bright orange chair with his head in his hands. I figure he's probably pretty angry about the bike. I try to reach out to him, but when I do, one of my arms feels really heavy and I can't get it to move towards him. I look at it. It's covered in a hard, white bandage and it hurts. It hurts really bad. I start to cry and my dad opens his eyes.

"What were you thinking? You could have been killed! And the bike is destroyed! Why can't you just listen? Why couldn't you just wait? Now you have to spend the whole summer in a cast. Jesus, Virginia, why can't you just behave?"

He's really angry and I know that because he used my whole first name. No one calls me Virginia. It's never felt like my name. Sometimes I sit and think of what my name should be and I never quite find it (I think maybe I haven't heard it yet) but I know it's not Virginia. Everyone calls me Ginnie. And that's not right either, but it's better than the other one.

He's also crying, like he's the one with a broken arm, not me. And I can't tell if he's more mad about me being hurt or the bike being broken, but I think it's the bike.

"I'm sorry I broke the bike."

He collapses into the bed and hugs me hard, too hard and it hurts my arm but it's better than him yelling at me so I don't say anything. And I don't think it was the bike after all. I think he was mad I'm hurt. Like I said, I make a lot of mistakes.

A nurse came in with a tray full of Jell-O and a cheese sandwich. My dad jumped away from me and his voice got weird and deeper. Like a tough guy in a movie. But my dad wasn't a tough guy.

The nurse looked at my dad. In the early spring me and some of the other kids from Mrs. Tonneman's first grade class found a bird on the sidewalk. It wasn't dead, then, but it was dying. It was so small and none of us knew what to do. So we just watched it breath, until it didn't breathe anymore. Then the bell rang. Mrs. Tonneman said it had probably fallen out of a tree and its mom couldn't help it. The nurse looked at my dad the way we looked at that bird. Maybe because she knew he didn't have my mom to help him.

She walked over to my bed and set down the tray. She was pretty, I thought. She looked like Snow White, but real, so her skin wasn't perfect, but she was nice. Her nametag said "Patty," and I thought that was a funny name. I wondered if anyone had called her hamburger. I decided not, since she was a girl, but if she'd been a boy then they definitely would have. Boys gave each other dumb names.

"I bet that hurts pretty badly," she said, and she smiled and I could see all her white teeth in a fine little row.

"It does. But my dad says I'm pretty tough," and I tried to show her by shaking my arm, but that really did hurt, so I stopped.

"I've got some medicine here that will help," and she handed me a small plastic cup of a red syrup that tasted like cherries. "But it will probably make you sleepy too. And that's ok. You can nap as long as you like."

I looked at dad and he nodded. He looked more like himself than he did before. So I closed my eyes.

"She's really cute," I heard her say to my dad.

"She looks a lot like her mother did," my dad replied. And I heard the way he said "mother" like he always did—like it was a word that didn't quite fit in his mouth and he had to work to get his tongue around it. I wanted to hear the rest, but my eyes wouldn't open and so I gave in and went to sleep. When I woke up my arm hurt less and Patty was gone and my dad loaded me up in the station wagon and we went home.

I spent the whole summer with a cast on my arm, which was kind of ok because the kids signed it and made decorations on it and I thought it kind of seemed like a knight's armor and that was pretty cool. I'd rather be a knight than a princess any day. The princess is always waiting on someone else to rescue her and she doesn't have any weapons at all. All you do is wait. I hate waiting more than anything in the world. That seems pretty boring.

Sometimes my room feels like a tower in a princess story. It was my mom's room, I guess, when she was little. It sits high above the lake and, if you squint your eyes, you almost feel like you're floating above it—like the gulls I watch in the morning. I know I'm supposed to be sad about my mom. I know I'm supposed to miss her and wish she were back. But how do you miss someone you never met? And, even if I did, it doesn't feel like she's gone. I feel her all around. Sometimes when I'm sad because of a dumb mean kid or I scraped my knee or I made another mistake and lost my ice cream after dinner, I swear I can feel her hand on my back. Maybe it's just wishful thinking. But even if it is, does it matter? I still feel it. I still feel her.

Dad showed me pictures once of her when she was little. At first I thought they were pictures of me and I wondered how my hair got so long. My dad likes to keep my hair short on account of how I'm always getting sticks and sand in it. My mom's hair was a long black rope, but aside from that I saw my own round face and big blue eyes. My grandpa always said I'd grow into my face. I don't know what that means. I suppose I'll find out.

In July Patty the nurse came to our house. I thought she was coming to make sure I hadn't gotten my cast wet. Twice a week my dad wrapped it in plastic so I could take a bath. I wondered what happened when you didn't wash your arm for two months. I bet it doesn't smell good. One time I left my gym socks in my backpack and then left my backpack out in the rain over the weekend. It was sunny when I opened the bag on Monday it smelled like the worst thing ever. I bet my arm smelled like that.

It wasn't easy not getting your cast wet when you live on the lake in the summer. Each day it got hotter and each day I went in a little farther—at first just letting the water wash over my toes as they sank into the sand. Then up to my knees and finally all the way up to my chest with my arm held as far above my head as I could. I ached to dive under. To feel the cold water lift my hair from my head and make it float around me and move in whichever way it chose. To see the little fish that swam on the clear bottom. It made me sad to think I wouldn't see them when they were little—by the time I could go under they'd already be big. I wondered why some things take so long to get big and others so little. So far I'd managed to outrun the waves and keep my cast dry with one exception.

I can't stay away from the lake when there's a storm coming in. Dad says, like all bad things, the storms come from Chicago. I don't know why they make storms in Chicago. They probably don't really because dad said it in that voice that means he means something else. When there's a storm you can see how far away it is and the far away part of the lake gets very dark and grey and sometimes green. And everything changes. The forest swells with noise, like a car revving its engine and then it goes completely silent. Completely silent is how you know it's time to get out of the water. I like how the forest tells you that. And it gets cold so fast. One minute you're sweating and your hair is stuck to your forehead and the next you wrap your towel around you and shiver. But my favorite part is the water itself. Normally the water is so cool and blue and flat and clean, but when the sky turns darks and the clouds get so big you can barely see the sky, the lake starts throwing things. It looks like how I feel inside when I get mad sometimes. That I want to throw my body at whatever I can until I'm not mad anymore.

I saw a magician once. My dad took me to the fair and there was a man in a top hat and a cape. He had a bunny in his hand. He put the bunny in the hat, waved a wand over it and it disappeared. I wondered if you could do that to people. I wondered if that's what happened to my mom. Then he pulled out a bright yellow scarf. He said some magic words and asked us to repeat them. And there, right before our eyes, the scarf changed to a deep purple.

That's what the lake is like. Like a magic trick. Only you don't see the magician. He's probably god, but I don't know because we don't go to church. But he makes people disappear and he changes the color of the lake, so it's probably him. The lake turns all of the colors at once—green and blue and black and grey and brown and white. And the waves go every direction at the same time—up and down and right and left. Like it's so excited it's about to rain it can't control itself. And I guess that makes sense because the rain came from the lake to begin with and now it's going home.

Most people run away from the lake when it looks like that, but I go towards it. Sometimes I stand on the shore and pretend I'm doing the magic. I was doing that last week when a big wave came out of nowhere and dragged me by the feet into the water. My first thought was that my cast was wet and my dad was going to be so mad at me. Then I remembered I can't swim with only one arm. I started to drift below the water and it was kind of nice being carried like that. Almost like being a baby and being carried to bed. It was almost like my mom was rocking me to sleep and I thought about that and kind of forgot that I needed to swim for a second. And I thought maybe I was like that bunny in that magicians hat, except I was me and the hat was the lake and maybe all the disappeared things go to the same place and my mom would be there too.

Then my butt hit the ground with a thud and I'd been washed ashore, but it had already gotten completely silent and that meant it would be raining by the time I ran up the dune home. I'd just tell my dad I made a mistake and stayed out too long and the rain got me. He's used to me making mistakes. He'd sigh a really long time and look like he was going to fall asleep or cry or maybe both and then he'd say "Ginnie, go to your room." And I would and later at dinner we'd both try and pretend I hadn't made another mistake.

Patty wasn't wearing her nurse's uniform. She was in regular clothes—a blue dress that looked as light as the wind. And dad was happy to see her, so I knew I wasn't in trouble. She looked different and dad looked like how my insides feel when I eat too much sugar. She came over for dinner every Tuesday and Thursday night and I thought it was nice dad had a friend. Plus he paid less attention to me, which meant I could shuffle more of my broccoli into my napkin. I wish we had a dog, Then I could just feed it all my vegetables. And meatloaf. I hate meatloaf.

I couldn't learn to ride a bike until my arm healed. The doctor thought that was ok and said I should spend the summer playing with my dolls. But he hadn't seen me since I was a baby so he doesn't know I don't play with dolls. I do climb trees. Sometimes I'll spend the whole day in a tree. My dad says he hates it, but sometimes, on good days, the days where he's saying what he means, I can get him to climb it too. And those are the best days.

So I learned to climb one-handed. I fell a few times, once on my cast and that hurt real bad, but I figured it out. And I spent most of the summer up there, pretending to be a knight and rescuing the princess. And that's where I was sitting when the mosquito landed on my arm. It wasn't the cast arm, but the other arm. I figured even a dumb mosquito is smart enough to know it can't sting me through a cast. I watched it as it landed. I wondered what it saw, where it had been that day. I wondered where I'd go if I could fly. I suppose I'd go flying over the water, like the gulls, so that my reflection and I could fly together. It would be nice to be alone, but not alone all at the same time.

I wondered what it would be like to be so small. People always comment how small I am (though the doctor said I'm basically right for my age) but a mosquito is so small you almost can't see it. I know what that feels like, though. Adults are always acting like they can't see me. Like kids are invisible. Except when they do something wrong. Then everyone can see them.

I wondered what it would be like to drink blood. I'd seen the steaks my dad brings home on Fridays and they are always dripping with blood in the see-through plastic sack Mr. Milovitch gives them to him in. But after they're cooked, there's no blood left. I wondered where it goes. It's not like how the water returns to the sky from the lakes when it's hot. Blood can't go back to where it started being blood. I don't know--maybe it can. There's so many mysteries in the world and so few people to tell me the truth about anything.

The mosquito doesn't care about anything else in the world though, probably. Just about me and here and getting a snack and not getting eaten by a bird. I watched closely as it lowered its weird mouth and stuck its needle face into my arm and its tiny body filled up fuller and fuller. At first it didn't feel like anything really, but then it started to kinda pinch and I got mad that it was eating me and I picked up my cast arm and crushed it.

I felt a little sad then.

Chapter 5

I'm being born again. It feels different and yet the same because I am starving. It seems no matter where or what you are born, we are hungry for something and we carry that hunger with us until we die. It's the great uniter—hunger.

I realize I need to escape the pod that's holding me and so I reach out to break it, but I find I don't have arms in the traditional sense. But my mouth seems like an arm, so I try that and find that it works nicely. I break a hole in the outer layer of what's confining me and peer out. I'm hoping there's food nearby.

I continue removing my outer shell for a bit, but am overcome with exhaustion and can no longer fight the urge to close my eyes and rest. I do. I do not dream.

I wake later and find my mother peering over what's left of my shell. I instinctively open my mouth and she feeds me. A chill has set in. Some part of me remembers it as a spring night in the dunes. The thought comforts me, but I'm shaking uncontrollably. My mother huddles myself and the others together for warmth. Fed and warm, I drift back to sleep.

Time passes oddly when you're a bird because flying doesn't obey time. You're up and down and right and left, but rarely just forward. Most of my time is spent looking for food because I am constantly hungry. My brain is nearly always occupied by the thought of eating or surviving.

I am out, once again, in the search for sustenance. The sun is so warm on my wings and the breeze is behaving nicely, allowing me to conserve my energy and focus on the task at hand. I hear insects nearby. My hearing is good and needed to hear the calls and warnings of other birds in danger or who wish me harm.

And I hear a song I have not heard before, but that I know as though it is my own heart. I do not hear the words, nor could I understand them in this brain, but the tune, the melody, the vibration of the animal making the sounds—those I know.

I follow the sound to a huge structure, the kind I know instinctively to avoid. I land on a railing and tilt my head to better locate the sound. It's coming from inside, but moving towards me. Every cell inside of me is urging me to eat, but something keeps me here. At least for a moment.

The primal part of my brain tells me to flee, but a need to hear the song keeps me frozen. The sound gets louder as it approaches and comes to an abrupt stop as the singer sees me. We look at each other, neither moving, neither afraid nor brave. Just there, in a moment, not sure of what the moment is. I try to sing the song back to her, it's a song I know, but I'm stopped by the limitations of the notes this body makes available to me. Still, she sings back. It's a game. She sings. I sing. We go on like that until I know I have to leave to try and eat before night moves in. I'll die if I do not. Yet it's still so hard to move. So I whistle once more and fly home.

We go on like this day after day. Some days she's not there to greet me, but most she is. She's started bringing me berries, which are my favorite and she leaves them on a small plate on the railing so that I can eat while I sing with her. She and I have a quiet understanding. We do not touch. But sometimes she gets so close I think she might reach out and grab me. To what end, I don't know. But, despite feeling a connection to her, I am a wild thing. And I must be left wild. Though I know I'll do whatever I can to visit this balcony often. To hear her sweet song.

A chill starts to set in and I can smell the decay of trampled leaves and grasses. Very little of the berries I normally find in excess are still hanging on bushes and those that are, are shriveled and dry. Something tells me to eat as much as I can. That soon I will be flying a very long way. I try to override the dna-provided blueprint, but I know I will lose this battle. I go to her one last time. We sing until I can sing no more.

Each day I fly until my wings might break, but something is pushing me onward, farther, further. Occasionally I see other birds, sometimes they are dangerous, but mostly I just continue on, trying to find the place my body wants to be. To fit myself into the empty place I can feel has been left just for me. To solve the puzzle. To be the piece.

I awake one morning to find a pull in my wings again. They tell me to leave the warm sun I sit in daily. They tell me to go home. To her. To the woods. To the lake. Home.

And I do.

It's incredibly cold when I arrive and though my body has slowly adjusted as I continued moving north, I half wonder if I've done it wrong. Others like me are scarce and I begin to wonder if I'm alone here.

I fly to her window. Each day. Always at the same time and she is always there.

As the spring moves forward and the days warm and the frost no longer sets the ground as hard as stone, I begin to notice fruit appearing in my nest. There's something else too. Something I remember, but cannot identify. Something put there by someone else inside of my very cells. What it's telling me isn't clear, but I know it's important. It feels like something I forgot to remember.

He appears.

Grey and yellow, a berry in his beak. Nature speaks and I listen. The past whispers and I obey. The future beckons and I heed its call.

I continue to visit her though my flight gets more and more weighted. I am heavier each day than I remember being the day before, yet it does not impede me greatly. Rather I feel like there is more of me, in a delightful way. Until one morning I awake and find my little nest full of eggs. Today I must stay. The girl will worry and I worry on her worry, but that worry is soon overcome by my immediate love of the warm, smooth round things beneath my feathers. I will try and go to her tomorrow, I think.

But tomorrow comes and goes, as do all days following. My chicks are needy and frail and I am unable to leave for much longer than what it takes to get food and the occasional addition to the nest, which is built into the base of a massive pine tree. I find that I do not want to leave. That I want to stay with them, here, forever.

Just as I have resigned myself to remaining here indefinitely, the chicks become plump and independent, just in time for the chill to set itself on the water again. I feel the pull south and realize I must go to her and say goodbye.

She is there when I arrive, as though she has waited an eternity. Her song is strong and excited, the notes not coming as smooth and relaxed as usual. I want to touch her. I want to take strands of her dark hair and weave them into my bed. I let her get close to me.

And then it is dark.

Chapter 6

My teacher told me to do it.

I told Mr. Pitchert about the bird last year in Second Grade science class. We were having a lesson about Michigan birds and I told him I had a bird friend that came and sung to me all summer and then disappeared. He said it had probably migrated, which means flying south when it's cold. That seems like a good idea. Winter is awful here, except for sledding and hot chocolate. Those are good, but I could still probably live without them.

He asked about the bird and got out a special book that could tell me what kind of a bird it was. I told him how she (at least I felt like it was a she) had feathers the color of the sky on a January day, but her belly was the color of the sun in August.

There was a picture of her in the book. It looked exactly like her. But Mr. Pitchert said most birds of the same kind look almost identical. I think it would be boring to look exactly like everyone else. There's a set of twins in my class and they look exactly like each other. They dress the same way, and the only way you can tell them apart is by asking if they like strawberries. Stacey does, but Stephanie doesn't. That's how you know who's who.

I'm glad I'm not a twin.

The book says the bird is called a Kirtland's Warbler. Mr. Pitchert says there used to be a ton of them, but then all the trees got cut down and now there are only a few. Before I was born some people planted some more trees to try and bring them back, but the trees are still little, so we'll have to wait until I'm an adult to find out if it worked.

It's weird to think I'll be an adult some day. It seems awful.

I waited all winter for her to come back. And then, in the Spring, she did. I sang to her and she sang back and I was so happy to see her I cried a little bit and my dad was worried about me but he didn't need to be because I had just missed her was all.

My dad was worried a lot lately. I'd gotten used to Patty being here. I think my dad did too. She was here all winter and he seemed happy enough, but happy like when you want to eat more cotton candy but your tummy hurts. I liked her. It was nice to have another girl around. She taught me how to braid my hair and told me fun stories about people at the hospital.   But around Valentines Day she came over and she was crying and dad was crying and that made me sad too so I cried. When I asked my dad where she went and if she was coming back he just said that sometimes people love each other but can't be with each other. I still wish adults would say what they mean. When I'm an adult I'm going to be very clear about what I mean at all times and especially to kids because they get so confused.

The bird left and Patty left and it was just me and dad.

I learned some more about my mom from my grandma. She was pretty and smart and "sarcastic." I didn't know what sarcastic meant and grandma laughed and said that I should because I was. Again, adults.

I still couldn't miss her though. I tried. But you can't miss someone you never knew. Or a feeling you never felt. I did miss the bird and I felt bad I missed it more than my mom who was dead and that was sad.

I got a new pair of shoes for school back in the fall. Dad let me pick them out. I was lucky my school didn't have a uniform like my cousin Marci's. At Marci's school she had to wear a skirt and burgundy socks up to her knees and a white shirt that looked like it itched. My grandma said she looked "darling," but I thought she looked miserable. Adults are always seeing things wrong. I did envy the way her hair was always flat and smooth, but she still had a mom so that was probably why.

We went to the store and I saw them. Sneakers, black and white, with bright white laces and a white rubber toe. The man at the store measured my foot on this weird metal ruler. He told my dad they had my size but that the shoes were meant for a boy and pulled out a maroon leather pair with a pretty little strap and flowers cut into the top. They were fine and I didn't hate them, but they didn't feel right. They felt like a lie I was telling someone. Kind of how sometimes when my dad is real sad in the car but then he gets out and he smiles at everyone and his voice sounds like an advertisement on the radio. I wouldn't have fought my dad on it—but my dad suggested we get both pair so I could sometimes wear the nice shoes (like on picture day) and sometimes wear the sneakers. The man at the store looked like he wanted to say something but then swallowed a bug or something real quick and couldn't. Maybe he realized I didn't have a mom. People look that way a lot when they realize I don't have a mom. People are constantly about to say something, but no one ever does. I wonder a lot about what they'd say if I did have a mom. Maybe it's not nice things. Maybe it's better this way.

Most of the year had come and gone and I'd worn the nice shoes exactly twice and the tennis shoes so much that there were holes where the canvas met the rubber and ink pen doodles on the toes from when I got bored in math. I like math now. But I hate how the teacher teaches it. Like we're supposed to hate it before we even know what it is.

I kept the shoeboxes. I like the way they looked. The squareness of them, the odd permanency of them even though they were meant to be trash. At Christmas I took one of them and cut pictures of cars out of magazines and arranged them artfully on the box. Then I glued them on and gave it to my dad for him to keep his ties in. He said he loved it. He didn't know I'd chosen the fancy shoebox, which was the one I liked least. I didn't figure he'd mind.

But I kept the other box. And I knew what I was keeping it for.

So when she showed up in the spring, I was ready. Usually birds don't let you get close. Except geese, which we have a ton of. They'll let you get to close and then scream at you and peck at your legs. And it hurts. One time Stacy Madigan and I found a goose nest on the playground. All we saw were the eggs. They were so big and the nest was so beautiful that Stacy picked one up. As soon as she did a huge goose landed on her head and started pecking at her hair and her face. Stacy reached up to cover her eyes and dropped the egg. I always thought that was weird. The mama bird was trying to protect her baby bird, but Stacy had to drop that egg. Otherwise she would have been hurt real bad. If the goose had just left us alone, we woulda put the egg right back in that nest. Maybe moms aren't as smart as they look in magazine advertisements.

But this bird let me get close. We sang for a bit, but I was so excited that my song sounded kind of funny, like I'd been running right before we started. My heart was beating real fast too. I put my hand out super slowly. She looked at it, looked at me and hopped right onto it. She weighed almost nothing. And she was so close I could see every individual feather, each one slightly different from the last, her yellow feathers so bright they looked fake. For a moment I just looked at her and it seemed like she was looking at me too. Then, as quick as I could I put her in the box, and used a thick rubber band to keep the lid shut.

The next morning I took the box to school. We get extra credit for bringing science stuff in for show-and-tell and I figured this bird, a bird that was rare, would be worth double.

I wore my good shoes.

It seemed like forever before Mrs. Irene called my name. Before me, someone showed a boring shell they said they got from a trip to an island in Florida, but I saw those shells all the time on the shore by my house. But Brian lied about a lot of things, so I guess that wasn't really a surprise. One time he said his grandpa was president of the United States but we looked it up at the library and he lied. He lies even when you can prove the truth and I think there's something kind of sad about that. Carrie Mueller went next. She had a wooden shoe her grandma brought back to her from a trip to the Netherlands. I couldn't imagine anything being worse than wearing wooden shoes. You'd make so much noise and they couldn't possibly be comfortable. You'd never get away with anything. And you definitely couldn't climb a tree.

Next it was my turn. I stood in front of the room and told them the whole story about the bird. Then I opened the box. But the bird didn't fly out.

At first I thought she was asleep. Her little eyes were closed and her wings tucked tightly on either side of her body. I poked her with my finger. But she didn't move. And she didn't wake up. Mrs. Irene made me throw it in the trash in front of the whole class.

And I was so mad. Not at myself. Not at Mrs. Irene. But at the stupid bird. Why did she let me put her in the box? Why did she die? I cried so hard I had to throw up and Mrs. Irene sent me down to Nurse Teresa and my dad was called to come pick me up.

My dad said it was a mistake.

I make a lot of mistakes.

Chapter 7

I'm being born again. I'm starting to enjoy the feeling—a mix of fear and hope and exhaustion. The truth is, you know at birth that you have no control over whether or not you'll be born. You can feel it's entirely out of your control. But it's not scary. It's just exactly what it is: a thing that's happening to you that has nothing to do with you. And, since you're temporarily caught in between two worlds, for a brief moment you can see both in and out of life. It's so beautifully distracting you don't care where you end up. It's only after you take your first breath. After you open your eyes and take a look around you, that you realize you'd like to stay here more than anything you knew you could want. And that's when you start holding on so tightly that you strangle, in so many ways, the life you've been given.

It's warm and I'm hungry and the sense that I'm connected to the universe through my connection to my mother, who is merely just a collection of cells and energy, is strong. I feel completely held and cradled in the universe's minds eye. I am nothing and everything, all at once.

But birth must happen. It's a promise that's been made and it must be kept. How it ends is irrelevant. That it will end is not. So I float towards fate, or am pulled by it, and enter the world. My immediate thought is of her. But it is completely negated my need to find warmth, comfort and food. I cannot see. My eyes remain shut and will not open. But my nose sees everything. I can smell in a way that is so clear it creates a picture of all things near me. I smell my mother and make my way close to her. She is warm and smells of exhaustion. I latch on to her instinctively. I am less helpless than I have been. I am further evolved. I am also, happy in a way that my emotional maturity could not allow previously.

I want to think more on these thoughts, but with each suckle I am pulled closer to sleep. It's funny that one of the first acts of living is the cousin of death. It's too much to take all at once.

With my eyes already closed sleep is inevitable. It grabs me in its dark embrace and whispers me to sleep. I obey. And it is the first good sleep I can remember.

■■

I am a dog. Now that my eyes are open and I see my brothers and sisters, my dogness is undeniable. I want to consider this. To figure out how to find her, but there's so much to learn and it takes so much of my energy to learn it. It's an odd type of energy—where I have so much at points I feel as though I'll burst—but then, without warning I get hit with a wave of exhaustion. I'm taught daily by my mother, who fiercely defends us and shows us right from wrong. I play with my siblings. We play hard and then collapse, en masse, into a pile of sleeping pup.

I know where I am because my nose tells me. I am the same place I have always been, but I've never seen it like I do now. My nose smells the water, but it almost smells the color of the water, smells how quickly or slowly the water is moving, smells what boat has been on it. It smells the sand, but it smells each granule individually. Which ones are made of polished stone from the land and which were carried from far away and settled here. It's an odd thing to smell history. I smell too the trees, what kind they are, their age, which animals call them home. It's like smelling through time but also in time and also the next time. It's like flying, but with your nose.

I grow constantly. It happens so quickly I can feel myself expanding. Feel my bones stretching, feel my skin fitting more tightly. The space between my bones shrinks and I am able to manipulate my legs and paws more easily now, struggling less and less to run, jump and walk.

My mother is a big, warm pile of patience. No matter how hungry we are, how greedily we approach her swollen undersides, she acquiesces and even seems to be made whole by the process. I am torn by the need to be near her always, and the intense desire to explore this world, which I already know, but have never seen from this vantage point.

When I sleep, I dream. I dream of her. I dream of us, together. Sometimes in the dream I carry her with me, not as an infant, but as one. As a single organism, sharing the same space. Other times I dream that we are both children caught in an eternal game of playing tag and each time I reach her she pulls away just at the last moment. Other times I dream of rabbits. I am still a dog, after all.

I grow some more. And so do my brothers and sisters. I can feel their weight on me when we wrestle—so much more solid and muscular, so much more in control of their bodies. We push each other hard, figuring out limits, setting rules wordlessly. Using our sharp, pointy teeth, we nip and bite, showing each other where the lines are, helping set each other up for success at this life of doggyness. While we certainly grow exponentially from our birth-state, we do not, I notice, grow large. I can feel myself nearing my full size and yet the couch remains statuesque in front of me. It remains my Everest.

While I love the warmth and care of my mother, I have found nothing compares to the laps of people. Even as a human, in any life I have had, nothing, in any way, compares to being a dog in the lap of a human. The design seems so perfect; it can hardly be an accident. For I can curl my body into the smallest circle, resting just perfectly on the smallest of laps. And I can always find a lap. It's like I'm a heat-seeking missile and your lap is the intended target. It's impossible to resist—and, if I can get settled, impossible for the human to resist. You know when you've won—you feel their body relax, their heart rate drop. It's meditating without trying. It's beautiful and perfect.

But the humans are on the couch. Sometimes they will pick me up and place me on their laps. This is nice because there are no negotiations—an agreement is already in place. You will sit, I will sleep. We will be warm. And our hearts will slow together. But, often, a sneak attack is needed. You must reach them when they first sit down and convince them to stay there. And to do that, you must be able to scale the couch. Sometimes, if there's a pillow or book nearby it gives me just the right height to make the jump. But often I am left pleading on the floor, unable to scale such great heights. Convincing the humans to stay is a trick all dogs are born knowing and must execute at all turns.

All of the people here are pleasant. Each with their own smell, a combination of their individual pheromones and personal preferences. The mother smells like milk, rose perfume, pine cleaner and fatigue. The father a musty book smell, whiskey and oil. The son (who is my least favorite because he likes to hold me high in the air and swing me around) smells like grass and air and dirt and salt. And the girl, the baby, smells like powder and milk and joy. The baby is my favorite. Her little hands lack coordination and often find themselves wrapped around my long ears (and they do seem like especially long ears) but a lick on her skin and she giggles hard enough to let go. She often lies down on a blanket on the floor and naps for hours. And I fit so perfectly by her side, nestled in between the fat rolls of her arm and belly. We are so warm. And we dream together, my nose happily breathing in the soft scent of new life.

The winter comes and goes and it is early spring, as is evident by the clear skies and the cold morning dew. I'm so much better able to maneuver my body and my legs feel less like I'm operating a puppet from inside of it.

The house is full of weird energy today. Things are being put in boxes and taken outside. The mother is sweating more than usual but it's a pleasant smell, nicer than her perfume. When all of the boxes are put outside, there remains one last empty box. There are markings on it, but I cannot tell what they signify, if they signify anything. I miss being able to read. I am not able to think on this further because the moment I think it, I am picked up and placed in the box, along with my bothers and sisters. This is both exciting and scary.

The father picks the box up and we stick our heads through the top. It's fun to see the house this way, floating high above it, seeing it go by in a blur. It's like flying without any of the effort or risk. He opens the front door, which we have never been out, and walks us down the steps, which is good, because steps are a challenge for me. No matter how hard I try, I cannot seem to get them right. When he reaches the end of the steps, he sets us down next to the other boxes. Tables have been set up outside. My mother is outside as well and she saunters by, giving us each a loving sniff. It's been months since we stopped nursing and started eating real food and we spend significantly less time together as a pack. It's not for lack of love; it just seems to be the way things are. We all accept this with little more thought to the matter.

The sun rises in the sky and as it does, we are pet by hundreds of hands. Some reach into the other boxes and leave with an item from the house. I smell them all and the stories are intoxicating. Many have dogs or cats at home and carry them with them unknowingly on their pants or skirts. The children all reach their hands in our box, their little fingers excitedly grasping for us, rubbing our ears and laughing the best possible kinds of laughs. Children are like ice cream, you may prefer some to others, but in the end, you'd take any of them.

First, it's my brother who is chosen. And, as the day progresses, the box gets bigger and bigger as our pack gets smaller and smaller. While I will miss them, I am also jealous that they will have their own laps to rest on.

I am alone in the box. The piles of things in boxes has shrunken bit by bit and fewer and fewer stop by to poke their heads in looking for treasure. I have stopped sticking my head above the top of the box in search of free ear rubs. I lie down and let myself drift off to sleep, wondering where I will go or if I'll be kept, which wouldn't be so bad I suppose.

I sleep and I dream. I dream of her. We are together on the beach, sitting, our bodies making impermanent shapes in the sand. We watch the waves slowly roll towards us, threatening to tickle our feet, but stop just short of us and return to the center of the lake. Her hair, the color of the sand when it's lit through the trees, lighter and darker in alternate places, is lifted gently by the breeze, almost as though it's running it's hands through her hair. She smiles and holds her face up to a waning late afternoon sun. A seagull flies over the water, reflecting on itself and the wind tilts it sideways for a moment before it steadies itself. I'm taking in the smells. The deep, sweet smell of decaying woods, the wet, crustacean smell of the sand, the smell of her—and the smell gets so strong it feels real and it wakes me. For a moment I'm lost in time and not sure where or what I am. Then I remember sadly, that I am a dog in a box and I am terrifyingly lonely and missing her.

The scent remains, but it feels like a holdover from my visions so I don't immediately give it much heed, other than to let my heart break slightly more. But my senses don't let up. I set my paws on the top of the box to look out once again. The boxes have all but been cleared. There is only a cherry red bike and myself that remain.

And then there they are there. Seemingly out of nowhere, standing over the bike. They are talking to the mother and father, laughing and exchanging something. They begin to roll the bike away. I begin to whine, at first loudly, but then with more and more abandonment. She must see me. I must see her. And then I bark. I have never barked and the first one sounds timid and hoarse. But I do not stop. I see them pause and turn around. The father says something. The mother comes and picks me up out of my box. She begins to take me inside, but I wriggle free from her arms and I run, as fast as my squat legs will take me. I run to her. I jump up to her knees and lick her ankles. I am delirious from happiness. She bends down and picks me up. She puts her nose to mine and rubs her forehead on my forehead. She holds me tightly and I do not want to ever leave the crook of her arm. This is how we were meant to be together, nesting in each other.

Her father tries to take me, but she will not let me go. He points to the bike. I feel her tense up. The words they use are louder and sound much like my whining. They are pleading. I understand the word "no." I know what it means. She holds me tighter and it hurts but I do not care. Tears begin to stream down her face and I gently reach up and lick them away. Her father pauses. He bows his head. She walks away, the bike left behind, me under her arm. She never stops talking to me and I never get tired of her voice. I desperately wish I could talk back, but when I try a long silly howl comes out. It makes them both laugh. I decide that's good enough.

Home is my home. The place I've always been, always returned to. I know its layout immediately and run, as fast as I can to my old room, which I can smell is now her room. I jump on the bed. She jumps with me. She looks me in the eye. She tells me my name is Maggie.

My name is Maggie.

She pulls her body into a spoon and I curl up inside of it. She pets me, as the sun sets and turns the room all manner of pink and red and we doze off. I am home. We are home.

We are inseparable. All summer we play in the water, splashing and swimming, floating and warming our bodies in the sun. We spend the long hours playing games. She tells me secrets but I don't understand them. But I don't care. I want to be the keeper of her secrets. I sit by as she climbs trees. I whine when she gets too high, worried for her safety. I stick my nose in her hair, on her feet, in her hands. I revel in the presence that is her.

She looks in my eyes for a long time. Her gaze, full of love, but I see something else cross her face sometimes. Like when a cloud moves over the beach suddenly, presenting the negative image of what was there before. It worries me in the way I am capable of worry, but just as quickly it's replaced by the happy and content girl before me.

One late summer day, we get up in the morning like we always do—stretching together like part of the same pack—and it's already miserably hot. My little body loves the heat. I'll sit in a pile of sunshine until I'm baking, but this is nearly too much for me. She doesn't even bother to dress, but just throws on yesterday's swimsuit.

We walk down to the water. It feels warm, like a tepid bath, but it's still a relief from the heat. But there's something lurking. I don't know what it is, but something is there, waiting to do harm. My animal body twitches and seeks but can find nothing. Still, I want her to go home. I whine. I head back to the house trying to lure her. But she will not go. She sits, melted, slowly becoming the things she resembles.

I hear it long before she does.

It's far away, but moving quickly. It rumbles in a way you can feel inside your ribcage. It rumbles in a way that makes non-believers begin to wonder if there was a god.

I cannot get her out of the water. I am left with the knowledge that I am not strong enough to pull her out. One pull of the undertow and I'd be gone, swept to the bottom, washed up on the far edges of the lake. But I can feel the water gaining strength. Turning, unseen, deep in the dark, gathering its power, making plans.

My only option is to leave to get help. But that means being away from her, allowing for the fact that she could get sucked under long before I can get back. But it's all I have.

So I run. I try and run faster than the lake is strong. I feel the sand below my paws, but barely, because I'm flying. I get into the house and run to her father's room. I jump on him. I growl and whine and get him to the door. He follows to the deck. I run back to the beach.

She is gone.

He is there. He understands. Without hesitation he jumps into the water. Diving below the waves, searching for her.

There's a terrible moment where they are both gone. I run back and forth on the shore, frantic. I let out one long howl as my heart reaches capacity.

Then, they are there.

He carries her to the beach, turns her head to the side. I try and get close to her and he pushes me away. I realize I cannot smell her. The lake has washed her inside and out. She's not breathing. I butt the top of my head against the bottom of her foot. Her father pushes on her stomach.

And finally she moves. Her body undulates with the same ferocity of the water and she is breathing. She is back. I'm too excited to keep my distance. I jump on her chest. She hugs me tight. We all cry in our own way.

This girl is constantly at danger's doorstep. Most of my days are spent at her feet, which are busily trying to find what harm there is to get into. I am constantly there, nipping at her heels, like a sheep I've been sent to protect. I try and herd her towards safety, but she is quick to reroute herself, moving ever so quickly towards the next thing. Her father is distracted mostly. He loves her, clearly, but he seems to float near her rather than be a fixed object.

Though I miss her immensely, I'm happy when she goes back to school. At least there, trouble will be kept in check and at bay, in the safety, which I'm sure she sees as confinement, of school. Maybe the reason we spend most of our early years in school is to keep the bad out—to save us from ourselves. To keep the pointy things and the sharp things out of our reach for as many hours as possible. To give us something else to focus on rather than what harm we can cause ourselves.

For a long time it's just her and I. She tells me everything. At the end of the day we sit on her bed and she tells me that day's events. I can't understand most of the words, but her smell tells the tale for her. I smell the other children she was near. Her sweat tells me today was gym glass. I smell the metallic scent of the scrape on her knee from a game of red rover at recess. There's the meat from her sandwich and the eraser scent from her classes. She got in trouble on a lot of days. On those days she smelled even more like chalk.

But, as the year went on, we were alone less and less. Other girls arrived. And mostly, I was happy to see them. Some were full of cuddles and soft hands and rubs between my eyes. Others were afraid of me. I didn't mind that she saw me less, sought out my company less. Our days still ended exactly as they began. With me resting in the curve of her stomach, her arm draped over me like it was she that was my protector.

The summers were much of the same, swimming and climbing and lazily daydreaming on the beach. Each summer added more friends, some the same as ever, some new. There were boys now too, who mostly left me alone, but played rougher than the girls did. They were a nervous lot, both the boys and the girls, and they smelled like confusion and fear. I could not tell of what, but I was always on alert for anything that might harm her.

She grew so quickly, her face getting further and further from mine. I used to fit squarely in the round of her belly, but now there was room for another dog and even then maybe one more. I started to smell additional scents—a rose perfume, the tinny smell of eye shadow, the waxy scent of a lip-gloss. Her hair reached long down the middle of back, but still smelled the same as it always had. When I grew sad about her growth, I stuck my nose in it and tried to remember her as I'd met her. Tried to see her face as she reached into the box and pulled out a small puppy. Tried to remember how her hands were once just the right size to pet me, fitting easily within the confines of my head.

There were other things too.

She'd become a woman. On those weeks I cuddled closer to her, trying to ease her pain and her mind, trying to keep her warm through what seemed like fear and excitement.

One day after school I smelled another person on her lips. A boy—a boy I'd met before, who had always been nice to me and often threw the ball for me to fetch. Her pulse raced for a week. These were new types of danger that I had no control over, no way to stop or curb. I wished there were some way to talk to her dad. To tell him she's drowning—slowly—almost so slowly it would look like floating. They say a drowning person often looks like they are swimming. And before you know it, they're pulled under and they're gone.

If he won't parent, I will. I rip up her make-up. She is furious, but slightly amused. I rip up her posters. I chew and claw at her diary. One night she tries to sneak out through an open window, the moonlight setting her hair on white fire. I pull on her ankle, trying to convince her to stay. Then I bark until her father comes. He catches her just as she's running down the dune to the beach, a shadowy figure waiting there.

After that she has little to do with me. I've betrayed her and I've no way to explain I'm more than an annoyance. That, as always, I try to keep her safe.

It happens so suddenly I don't know what's happened. I am in the car. He rolls down the window and I stick my head out, smelling the warm air of early spring. I wonder where we're going. I haven't been in the car since they first brought me home and that seems like a very long time ago now. I'm not old, but I'm not a puppy either. I'm just a dog. He seems sad, but he always seems sad. I want to shake him, wake him up, make him enjoy the life he has. But I've no way to talk and he doesn't listen well anyway.

We arrive at a home. A little girl comes out and grabs me. She hugs and hugs and it's uncomfortable, but nice to be cuddled so fiercely. A woman comes out. She waves. I watch him pull away in the car and I understand.

She left me.

She outgrew me. I don't fit in her life anymore and I was never a part of his. It's funny how someone can once be your entire world and then, with no warning, you're replaced by someone or something else.

I'll never hear her secrets again.

I let out a long, slow howl as I let my heart break.

As soon as I can I run away and try to get to her. I need to see her. I need to hear her voice and smell her thoughts. I run, blindly, following my nose home. I do not think, I do not pause, I just let my soul guide me to my missing piece. And I'm running so fast, so urgently, that I don't even hear the car coming.

CHAPTER 8

I want a bike.

I'm almost in fifth grade and my dad still won't let me get a bike, even though everyone else in my class has one. Ever since I broke my arm trying to ride my mom's bike he won't even let me look at one. But without a bike I'll spend the summer walking the long roads to friends houses, watching my friends scoot effortlessly around, full of freedom. There's three weeks left of school and I've convinced him that if my report card is all A's he has to give in.

I'm pretty sure I'll get A's in English and science and math. It's history I have a problem with. For some reason the past won't stick with me. It's like my brain doesn't have the ability to move backwards, only forwards. So I'll learn why the south lost the war, but it immediately leaves my brain, leaving behind the residue of the memory, but a whole host of thoughts on how it affects the future.

My history teacher, Mrs. Kauffman, says learning the past is important so we can build a better future. Her family was in the Holocaust, and she says it's super important that never happen again. I agree with her. I just don't think we need to know the names and dates of every single little thing. Just the important parts. We learn history the same way we learn math, but I think we should learn it the same way we learn poetry. Like, what does it mean? What was the author trying to say? Mrs. Kauffman says we're all the authors of our own history, writing a new chapter every day, every month, every year.

I feel like the history book of my life started in the past and just stays there, unable to move forward or change. Like I'm the remainder in the difficult equation of my mom and dad. And my mom is a negative number because she doesn't exist here anymore.

I used to not notice her not being here. But a lot of the other girls are in Girl Scouts; their moms are the troupe leaders. And all they do is complain about how their mom's are everywhere. I'd like to tell them it's better than their mom being nowhere. But something tells me it wouldn't matter. That you can't see the negative of an image while simultaneously viewing its positive.

A lot of times I wish my dad had married another woman so I'd have some kind of mom. A step-mom is still a mom. Someone to take you school shopping and talk about boys and how Josie got her "period" and how that seems terrible because now she can get pregnant, but no one knows how, so we all just stay away from her in case we catch it. I saw her holding hands with Johhny Mancuso at lunch one day and if I had to guess I'd say that's how it happens.

I wonder what it's like to be pregnant. I put my pillow under my shirt, shaped like a big, lumpy belly and tried to imagine myself pregnant. It just felt weird and awkward.

I'm never having kids. It can kill you.

But there is a boy I like. And I think he likes me too. But it's so hard to tell because we can't make eye contact without one of us running away and usually running in to something. It's all so embarrassing it makes me wonder how anyone actually falls in love if you both look like idiots all the time. In movies no one looks like that. It's all moonlight and long walks and gentle but serious kissing. With us it's like high-fives and tripping over your book bag. So, I think, maybe it's not love. Maybe it's just how boys and girls are to each other. Either way, it's dumb.

It's Saturday morning and my dad and I are doing what we do every Saturday morning, eating cereal while I watch cartoons and my dad reads the paper. My dad is always reading the paper. One time in school we were supposed to draw our parents. My mom was easy. Every memory I have of her is a portrait. Her, frozen in time, slightly smiling, eyes bright, but unfocused. I just drew a picture of a picture.

My dad, I couldn't see his face in my mind. I saw parts of it, but it was like a Picasso painting—all messy and floating away from itself. I think it's because it's usually covered up by something. His hand, the paper...it's like he's trying to hide himself from me. I ended up just drawing a circle with a mop of brown hair. I got a B. Funny how someone who's dead is easier to see than someone who's alive.

So that's how we spend our Saturdays. I've got lots of friends who have Saturdays that seem so foreign to me—dance classes, roller skating, sports teams. I imagine their parents, busily guiding them and their siblings to activities, clapping when they score a goal, taking a photo at a dance competition. I sometimes see the early morning version—when I'm invited to sleepovers—and I'm aware that dropping me off is just one more thing on their parent's to-do list. These Saturdays seem so full and so loud and so...full of life, compared to our humble, quiet Saturdays.

While he was reading the paper that Saturday morning my dad noticed a posting for a garage sale, listing a bike that is just my size. He says we should go for a ride to check it out. I'm excited but nervous. It seems to come out of nowhere and, in my life, things can turn on a dime. I could make a mistake by the time we walk to the door and the whole thing could go up in smoke. It seems unfair that I have both no mother and terrible luck, but I guess some people just don't get an easy version of life. I guess someone needs to get the bad stuff or other people wouldn't know they had the good stuff. Although it seems like those people rarely know they have it anyway.

We hop in the wagon and head out. This is my favorite time of year, mostly because the trees are best for climbing. In the summer the leaves get too thick. In the winter it's just too cold, although jumping into piles of snow from the top of a tree makes the dark days go by a little faster. In the fall everything is brittle and dry and you're likely to break a branch and your neck. But in the spring the buds are just starting and you can see from the top for miles. The trees are bendy, but strong, taking in the rain and the sun. They are my favorite trees, spring trees.

As we drive through the subdivisions I see all the families, getting outside now that it's warmer, pushing bikes and strollers. I try to imagine what we might have been like if our house didn't feel like it was wearing a sweater all the time. All cold and fuzzy. I try to imagine it filled with laughter and light. I try to imagine my mom and dad, holding hands maybe, watching me splash in the lake. I try to imagine a photo album full of our lives—trips to places like the Grand Canyon. Maybe there would have been a sister or a brother to love and hate. I don't think on it much. I'm not "prone to drama" like Mr. Carnicki says Tess Gerber is. But on a day like today, it feels like I'm being asked to imagine it. Like a movie that's playing just for me. Like I'm on the outside of the life everyone else is living.

I turn away from it and watch my dad drive, trying to hold his face in my mind, but it keeps slipping and turning. He's there, but then he's someone else that looks a lot like him. I tend to think there's nothing you can hold on to for long—not with your mind or your hands. Like it's all made of water that's frozen for just a second and then it remembers what it is and washes away. Mr. Carnicki says I'm an "old soul." We don't take him very seriously because he teaches PE and his shirts are too small and his stomach sneaks out the bottom. Plus he collects mugs from different drive-in restaurants and one day he brought in the whole collection to show us, but he told us it was only half because "Helen got the other half." He didn't tell us who Helen was, but I don't think it's fair we didn't get to see the whole collection since he bought them all. But that's life. Me and Mr. Carnicki have some things in common.

"Old Soul" doesn't sound like a compliment even though Mr. Carnicki said it in a compliment voice. Adults seem to have different voices for everything and they usually don't match the thing their saying. No wonder they fight all the time. They're completely confusing. But "old" is never good. There are types of old that are good, I learned them in my "English for advanced readers" class. Antique, ancient, vintage—but old is just plain old. Old shoes, an old dog, old house, old person—these aren't great things. These are things that are no longer just what they are—they are now just old things. And they're all tired and worn out. I feel tired and worn out a lot. Not in my body, but somewhere else. Like in my mind, but not a thought or an idea. I don't know.

I know I don't think the way the other kids do. But then they have two parents and bikes and dogs and don't live in the side of a sand dune with a dad whose face won't stay put. So it's easy for them to just to think about bands they like and ponies and movie stars with handsome plastic faces. I keep hoping maybe that will be me someday. Just a kid, with no thoughts other than the ones everyone else is having.

My dad pulls over to look at the ad in the paper again. He's lost. He's kind of always lost, so it doesn't surprise me. A lot of times he'll walk into a room, stand in the door, and be still for a moment before saying, "Huh. Now why did I come in here?"

He gets lost in his own house, let alone a neighborhood he's never been to before. It's also kind of easy to get lost here. All of the streets have the names of trees—Poplar, Elm, Maple, Oak, Beech—it's kind of hard to keep them apart. And all the houses look vaguely familiar—like you dreamed them one time and they were your house, but also not your house at the same time. But they're not dreams; they're real with real people sitting in them, with someone baking bread and someone else putting a baby down to nap and someone else working in the garage. Houses are alive, even if they look like ghosts.

He can't find the ad, even though he borrowed my special pen with four colors to circle the words in the paper. He used the red, but I mostly use the green.. I take the paper out of his hand and point it out to him.

1919 N. Pine, it says. Another tree.

We head two blocks up, passing happy-looking people dressed in beige tracksuits walking beige dogs past beige homes with beige cars in the driveways. It's as if everyone bought everything in the same place. Even their hair is the same. Each one as milky blonde as the last, except the kids who have white parts in their hair from playing outside. But someday they'll grow up to have the same colorless hair as the adults. You can't outgrow genetics.

We learned that in science this year. We each got an egg assigned to us. They all looked the same. We put them in an incubator. I wondered if their mother cared we'd taken them away to perform some kind of experiment, replacing her body with artificial light. How sad to be replaced by something you can buy at the farm and fleet.

We set the incubator up in the middle of the classroom. We waited and took notes, pretending to be real scientists in the field, marking down temperatures and dates, noticing if there were any changes in our eggs. There was nothing special about my egg. It was just an egg, round and smooth and looking no different that the ones we bought at the store, aside from a lack of condensation from the humidity of our mustard-colored fridge.

But, I felt related to my egg. I couldn't help but name it even though the teacher said not to. Humans love to name things. In my notes it was EGG #16. But in my heart it was Hubert. Maybe it was my deep desire for a pet, for something of my own to connect to. I don't know.

I watched Hubert each day. Daydreaming about the adventures we'd go on. Wondering what color he'd be when he hatched. It bothered me a lot that we'd had to leave them in the school all alone over Christmas break. My mind went through a million terrifying scenarios all leading to the eggs and their insides being destroyed. Mr. Neihaus promised us that he would make sure the incubator was checked every day, but still, I spent my break worrying about Hubert. I barely even looked at the gift my father had gotten me. It was a scarf. It just made me worry that Hubert wasn't warm enough.

The first day after break I rushed into our classroom. Each and every egg still in its place, warm and cozy and all in one piece. I breathed out for the first time in two weeks. I decided to bring Mr. Neihaus some cookies from the next time I went to my Nana's.

A couple weeks later Sharon Stephens let out a loud squeal. We rushed over to find that one of the eggs had begun to crack. A tiny beak was sticking out. Our teacher explained hatching would go very slowly and we couldn't spend our whole day just watching the chicks try and remove their shells, even though we really wanted to. Over the next week every single egg had a beak breaking through. Some chicks got themselves free and basked in the warmth of the lamp, looking exhausted and frail. Within a day they looked bright and fluffy and hungrily ate up the feed we threw in their habitat.

I couldn't stop thinking about how much work it is to be born. It seems like you blink and you're just alive, but that's not it at all. You have to work for it. I wondered if they missed their mom. It seemed cruel to do so much work and have no one tell you good job when you arrived, healthy and tired.

Hubert took longer than the others to arrive. I figured he was just taking his time, making a grand entrance. I figured, like me, he was a little different from the others. One morning I walked in as class started and the whole class was gathered around the incubator. They were being quiet, which wasn't like them at all.

I joined the pack. And I saw Hubert. Half still in his egg and half out, he was scrawny and smaller than the others and he was not moving. I said he was sleeping. But my teacher just reached in, grabbed his tiny body and threw him in the trash. He said that not all the animals make it. It's nature's way of making sure the strongest of the species survive.

I spent the rest of the day looking at that trashcan. Thinking about how hard life is to make and how easy it is to dispose of.

I guess we all weren't meant to live.

I haven't eaten eggs since.

My dad finds the house from the paper and we get out. I see the bike. It's red and shiny and everything I could have hoped for. I can see myself joining the gangs of other kids. Doing tricks on its seat and feeling the wind rushing passed my face. Tasting the water it's heavy with on the days when the air and the lake seem like the same thing.

It's a boy's bike, but I don't mind. Why they make different bikes for boys and girls is a mystery to me. We use the same parts, legs, arms, butts—the bike doesn't care what the differences are. It only knows to go when pedaled, stop when told. There's a sign on it that says $20. Around it are the remains of the garage sale. Empty boxes, assorted loose books, and basket full of antique handkerchiefs. Some kids play in the yard. They don't seem to care that their stuff is laid out for us to pick through, like the scavenger birds I learned about in science this year. Hawks and falcons and crows, looking for whatever scraps they can find. I think of Hubert again and imagine a hawk picking him apart. In hindsight I'm glad he ended up in a clean trashcan.

My dad searches for his wallet. I know he's left it on the dashboard. It's a habit he has. He gets in the car, gets back out, takes his wallet out and sets it in the dashboard. He forgets it there often. But he also forgets he forgets it's there often. I could tell him, but I'm enjoying how different this Saturday is. The different people, sights and smells—where dad and I are doing something together. Almost connected, or at least as connected as he and I get.

Eventually he figures it out and walks over to the car. I'm running my hands over the bike, feeling its cold metal frame, admiring the way the welder bent and shaped and connected. Admiring the way the painter got every square inch and chose a candy apple red with little flakes of fire inside. Admiring the barely used tires and the pedals I can't wait to have under my feet. In the background there are lots of sounds. The rush of cars, people talking, the kids playing, a barbeque across the street, dogs barking. The barking sounds insistent. It sounds like any other dog's bark, but also different somehow. Like the dog is trying to form a sentence, trying to talk to someone. I go back to the bike, lost in love for this object. But the barking won't leave me alone. It's full of some combination of joy and panic and getting closer.

It's so close now I don't understand where the dog could be. That's when I see her. She's at my feet. A tiny little ball of happy that I know is named Maggie.

I pick her up. She licks my face with such overwhelming excitement that I can barely open my eyes. I love her immediately and without question. I hold her close to me and she tries desperately to decrease the space between her body and mine.

It doesn't take much for dad to understand what has happened when he returns. He says no before his mouth even forms the words, but it's too late and he knows it. I will not leave without her. I will stand here, on the lawn of this house in this neighborhood for an infinity before I will let this dog go. I'm crying already, even though I know I will win this battle because I've already won it just by finding her. I love her in a way that doesn't make sense. She reaches up with her tiny puppy face and cleans my tears away.

My dad offers me a choice. It's the bike or the dog. I don't even look at the bike. I just start walking to the car, Maggie in my arms.

When we get home she races in, directly to my bedroom and onto my bed, as though she knew where it was. I'd expected her to explore the house, but she seems to know it already, or at least be comfortable not knowing. We snuggle on the bed and I look into her eyes and tell her her name over and over again. Without a sister or a mom she's the first girlfriend I've truly had. I tell her everything. I tell her about school, friends and enemies, teachers I love and teachers I hate, I tell her about Hubert. Over the weeks and months I tell her every dream and every nightmare, every frustration with my dad, every hope for the future. I hadn't realized I talked so little until I had reason to talk so much. Once I start talking I can't stop, like someone took the cap off a shook-up two-liter of pop. It just keeps fizzing up, doubling in size, full of force seemingly from nowhere.

And she is the best listener. She sits attentively, curled up in the sun or the warmth of my stomach. My lap is her lap. It's real estate she owns now. Her tiny ears stand up straight when I talk, her eyes never leave mine. Her shiny fur feels so soft and warm that sometimes her nearness makes me sleepy and sometimes, even though I'm way too old for naps, I'll find myself drifting to sleep while talking—a story interrupted by a dream.

On the last day of school when the other kids are headed off to camp, for the first time I do not feel left out. I have something to do. Something to spend my summer energy on.

And the summer is ours. We own the lake and the beach and the trees and the heavy rains. We eat juicy peaches and blueberries from nearby farms and they are somehow twice as delicious as I can ever remember them being. We run up and down the dunes, her almost disappearing into them. Like losing a copper penny in the sand. When I climb my favorite tree she sits at the bottom, waiting and whining, getting smaller and smaller as leaves and branches go passed me. If I climb high enough and sit for long enough she'll eventually give up her fear and curl up at the base of the tree, in a patch of mottled sunlight, and give in to a well-earned nap.

The summer is so hot. At night I hear the weatherman on the news say it's the hottest summer we've had in 100 years. I wonder what was where my house was 100 years ago. My climbing tree, my dad says, is 100 years old. I wonder what it's seen, though I doubt the forest and the lake have changed much in 100 years. That's the funny thing about nature, things die all the time, but it keeps making more. And one chipmunk looks like another chipmunk if you're not looking closely, so it just seems like there's always been a chipmunk there. I wonder why people aren't the same. Why, when my mother died, she wasn't replaced by another woman, who looked and sounded exactly like her. That seems like a much better design.

Humans don't let nature do its job. Maybe that's why we're different. Maybe we're somehow punishing nature for the fact that we weren't built the same. Or maybe it's the other way around. Maybe nature takes us away from each other as payback.

My dad told me the woods around our house used to be older and bigger and more wild and the dune wasn't there at all. Then, like 100 years ago, Chicago had a huge fire. I think a cow started it. Maybe nature sent a cow to set fire to the place. Maybe the cow was taking revenge on Chicago since they were famous for murdering cows. I like the idea of a cow superhero. I imagine it sneaking (very hard for a cow to sneak) into a barn, and kicking over a lantern, then freeing the fellow cows and out-running the people.

Anyway, since a lot of people lived in Chicago, they had to rebuild all the buildings and the houses and the barns and since they already used all their wood, they came and took our trees. And when they took our trees, the wind and the water crushed down what was left into a fine golden sand and made the dunes. Dad says the dunes are actually bad for the lake, but I think they're kind of pretty. But a lot of animals lived in the woods and they all lost their homes. So a few years ago people replanted a lot of the trees and stuff and some of the animals came back. So maybe people are learning their lesson? Maybe we're trying to make it up to the world? Maybe if we try hard enough we won't lose people that we love.

We don't go to church, but I went once when I slept over at Bridget McMannis' house. Her family is Irish Catholic, they told me, and we got up early to go. I didn't have anything to wear, so I borrowed one of Bridget's dresses. It was too tight and it itched, but her mom told me I looked "like a lady." Why you need to dress up to impress someone who has no body makes no sense to me. And my grandpa says that anyone who judges you by what you look like isn't worth knowing. I wasn't sure about this Catholic "God" guy already.

We all piled into her family's sedan. Her older brother Don was two years ahead of us in school. He had bright red hair. He always said he hated it, but I thought it looked like a sunset on his head. Like he was always having a beautiful idea and it just floated there for everyone to see. Plus, he was handsome. I'd seen a lot of photos in their house of President Kennedy (they told me he was the most famous Catholic outside of the pope) and I thought Don was handsome in the same kind way. Like he belonged pulling the ropes on a sailboat. Like he should always be in khakis and a cable knit sweater, easily rolling with the waves of the lake no different than if he were standing on land. I figured if church were that unbearable, I could always just look at him. Or at least be near him and his hands, freckled by the sun. When he saw me in Bridget's dress he punched me in the arm and said I looked ok. I nearly fainted.

The church was bigger than I'd imagined. From the outside it looked almost quaint. Like a chapel in one of the fairytale books that were handed down to me from when my mom was a girl, living in the same room I do now. I still open those books sometimes and admire the beautiful drawings, their bright crimsons and muted blues all tinted yellow. The princesses so fair and thin and the knights so brave and silver. They always got married in a chapel that looked exactly like this one. But on the inside it was so echoey and cold it took my breath away. I'd always heard that God was love. But this place felt like a prison. Maybe that's what religion is—a beautiful prison. A place where you're kept without wanting to be free. And it was so cold. Stone floor to ceiling with the exception of the long, hard wooden benches and the stained glass windows. The widows had images of a man carrying a cross. His face looked tired and sad. It was a beautiful day outside and I suddenly wished more than anything to be in my tree. I couldn't understand why these people would separate themselves from the thing God made for them. He was right there. In the trees and the water. Right there. In the birds and the sky. He was so totally touchable, not locked away in dark places. He was in Don's hair when the sun touched it and made it brighter than before.

The priest talked a lot about death. I guess you're supposed to want to die because that's where heaven is. I wondered if that's where my mom was. I didn't think so though because she felt so close all the time. How could she be way up there and yet sometimes I knew she was right next to me? I guess she could be an angel, but I couldn't picture her with big wings and glowing at the edge of my bed. She didn't seem like the kind of person who'd want to be an angel anyway. She smelled like the ground. Like cold earth. Like a combination of everything that's ever been in that place, all mixed together. I never understood calling someone dirty, because dirt is the best smell ever. Maybe you only understand that if you live in the north and you don't get to smell it for half of the year. Or maybe there's different smelling dirt. But here it smells like the lake and home. And I'd rather be near the dirt than in heaven with a god who wants me to waste my Sunday sitting on a bench that's hurting my butt in a dress that makes my skin feel like its on fire. So, I think I'll try and stay alive as long as I can.

After church they drop me off at home. I watch Don out of the corner of my eye the while way home, just because it makes me happy to see him enjoy the wind blowing through his hair.

The summer is aggressive in its heat. I don't even bother taking my swimsuit off for days at a time, only giving in when I develop a rash from not washing off the lake and the sand for too long. It's as hot in the morning as it is at night. It feels like it will never end. I wonder what that would be like. To just know that the weather will remain the same day in and day out. I guess you'd get used to it. Kind of like how I'm used to it being 90 one day and 30 just a month later. I like it that way though.

I get out of bed and it's still humid. My dad says when I was little I called it "human" because I misunderstood what he said. It does not feel human. It definitely feels humid. I try to get out of bed, but my legs are being held captive by a rust-colored ball of heat. I shake her a little. She will not move. She loves to sleep. So do I. We're good together like that. I call her name gently. Her tail moves just a little. Just the very tip. Her ears pop up and towards me. Like she wants me to know she hears me, but also wants me to stop talking. It's a lot what I probably look like in the winter when dad is trying to get me up for school.

I roll away from her and she pops up and onto the floor. When she stretches it looks like she's bowing to her queen and I curtsy. The windows are open. The sky is grey all the way across the lake. There's a storm somewhere and I wish it was here. Everything is so much better after the rain than before it. Right now the air is so heavy and thick it feels like you're walking through bath temperature water. It's hard to breath. Sometimes I spend the day in the trees, pretending I'm in the jungle. Michigan is so far from being a jungle, but on these days, with the wet breeze and the thick air, if you squint your eyes a little you can pretend the squirrels are monkeys and the vines are huge man-eating snakes.

But today I just want to swim. Just float in the water til the rain comes and washes me to shore. It's too hot to sleep and too hot to be awake, so swimming will have to do. I've still got my suit on from yesterday so I walk to the laundry room to grab a clean towel.

There are no clean towels.

My dad says I'm old enough to help with things like laundry and I know he's right but I hate doing it. I know kids who have chores –like taking out the trash or raking the leaves—but none of them have to do laundry. They all have moms that do laundry. Except Becky TenHarmsel. Her mom works as an ATTORNEY, and wears suits and high heels and stuff and she takes her clothes to the dry cleaner. So, I guess her mom still takes care of the laundry.

I wish my mom were here to do laundry, but then I think that's a terrible reason to want a mom. Why would she want to be here if she had a daughter that just wanted her around so she didn't have to do chores? I reach into a pile to grab a load to put in, but Maggie is laying on top of it already back asleep.

I pull the towel out from under her and she topples to the floor, rolls once, gathers herself and stretches again. Then she sits and stares up at me, waiting for me to lead her to the next thing. I grab a towel and smell it. It smells like the lake and the sand and a dog and a little bit moldy. I figure another day at the beach won't hurt it. I tell Maggie we're going to the beach. She wags her tail at me. I could tell her we were walking to our deaths and she would wag her tail at me. I guess that's kind of nice.

The water is warm and I feel better instantly. Normally Maggie walks back and forth along the edge, getting herself a drink here and there and then she curls up on the towel and sleeps. At the end of the day she smells like she's been baked, which I guess she has. But today she looks different. Her little body is tense and she won't stay with me. She whines and she barks and it's so hot and I'm tired of it, so I swim out further than normal just to get away from the sound. I dunk my head under and let the noise into my ears. It's funny how the lake can be so quiet one moment and so loud the next. You can be standing, right on the shore and hear nothing at all. But underneath the flat water it is louder than anything you've ever heard. It says a lot about how you look at things. Sometimes I feel like I spend my whole life above water, but I'm so much happier when I go under. When I use my body and make it feel. Put pressure on it. Get smaller than something else.

Adults seem to spend a lot of time trying to be bigger than everything else. And everything has to be comfortable. Chairs, beds, cars, and clothes—I'm not even sure anyone feels their bodies at all. Like we're trying to forget them or pretend they aren't there. Maybe they remind us that we won't have them one day. That one day we'll wake up and never go to sleep again.

I can still see her racing along the shore, barking her head off. I can see the storm coming, but it's still in Chicago. There's no lightening. I can barely feel the water against my skin because they are so close in temperature. Sometimes I hate living so far away from everyone else, but on days like today I'm so glad to not have to go to a public beach with my friends. I've done it. It's terrible. You get in a hot car, your legs sticking out of your swimsuit and onto the nearly melted vinyl of the seats, you roll the windows down, but it makes no difference. Then you drive to the hottest parking lot in the world and try not to burn your feet as you race down to the waterfront because there is no shade because they took all the trees away. And there's 700 other people trying to do the same thing and the birds steal your food. It's no way to be happy.

I start to feel bad about Maggie so I swim in to calm her down. But two strokes in I feel something grab my leg. Like a rope. I reach down to move whatever it is off of my ankle, but there's nothing there. There's always stuff in the water floating by. Lots of old ships are on the bottom of the lake, preserved forever, home for fish. Another stroke in and the thing grabs me again, this time dunking me under the water. I feel my belly flip in fear. I kick harder, but the rope tightens and I'm being pulled further from the shore. I get my head above water for seconds at a time, grasping for things that aren't there. I don't know where the lake is taking me. Somewhere in the distance I can hear Maggie bark and howl. Then the sound is gone because I'm deep under water. So deep that it's a lot darker here. I stop panicking for a moment and look around. I've stopped fighting for air and I wonder if I'm dead already. Or if maybe this is where I belong. It's so beautiful under here and I don't mind being alone. I wonder if I'll see my mom. I wonder if she's here now.

I close my eyes and let sleep take me over.

In the dream my mom is here. She floats below the water, moving as it moves, shifting color as the rays of light from above move through her. She is more beautiful than I'd ever imagined. And young. She's so young we look more like sisters than mother and daughter. I feel happy and calm and glad to be here with her. She reaches up and gently touches my cheek. For a while we just stare at each other. I have so many things I want to ask her, but we're underwater and I can't seem to open my mouth to form words. But it feels like she's here to wait with me. Like when you're big enough to go into the doctors room alone to get your shots, but your dad sits with you anyway. Maybe she's here to take me with her. I think about that. I was kind of looking forward to growing up and doing some grown up things. But I'm also more tired than a fourth-grader should be. Maybe I am an old-soul after all. But I would like to get to know my mom. And she looks so beautiful and so full of peace it's hard not to want to go with her.

She hugs me. And she's so light and slender I expect her to go right through me. But her arms float around me. At first I feel warm and happy. Like I'm dissolving into her, the two of us becoming one specter. But then she's squeezing too hard and I can't breathe again. It's like I'm drowning in reverse. I struggle to get free of her release, but she's so strong and I'm too weak. If I don't get free she'll crush me and I'll die inside of death.

The water is coming up hard, shaking my body, torturing it with convulsions. I breathe air. I open my eyes. Something is pressing on my feet. I see my dad. He is so scared and looks so young and I suddenly feel a great deal of pity for him. Then I feel sad myself because I realize she's gone. My mom is gone. She's dead. She's always been dead, but her second death feels worse than the first because I'm old enough now to understand it. I try to cry but the inside of my body hurts so badly I'm just making sounds like an injured animal. Maggie leaps on my chest and I hold her as tight as she'll let me. I don't want to crush her. I know what that feels like, but right now I can't feel what's too much or too little. The whole world feels barely there, like it could open up and we'd fall through to nowhere. Just millions of particles living in between other particles. I guess that's all we really are. I cry for my dad. I cry for my mom. I cry for a dead duckling. I cry for myself. I was empty already, but when I'm done, I'm like a whole new person.

I feel the wet sand on my back. I want to be in my bed, but I realize leaving this place means leaving her. I want to be in the in-between world for as long as I can. But my dad stands up and lifts me. I'm too tired to fight him and it feels good to have arms around me again. I shut my eyes and sleep, warm and safe.

Things afterwards are different. My mouth tastes like dead seashells and there's no end to the amount of sand between my teeth. Even weeks after, even months after. And nothing looks right. Everything is hazy like you're looking though waxy glass—distorted and foggy. There, but almost dreamlike. I can still make out the shapes and colors, but they're less permanent, less real. A real time illusion that only I can see. I'm taken to a doctor who looks in my eyes and tells my dad the lack of oxygen to my brain may have caused some damage to my eyes. But there's nothing wrong with my voice, he says. My voice is fine.

He assures my dad of this because I haven't spoken in months. It's not that I can't. It's that I don't know what to say. There seems to be nothing left to say. Maggie is the only one who seems not to care. She doesn't need an explanation. I am still the same warm body I always was.

But I feel less warm. My hands and feet are always cold. No matter how much I rub them they stay chilled from the inside out. Even wearing gloves inside and two pair of socks does nothing. Because part of me died. I know that. I don't know how to explain that, but it happened. It did. And I could have died all the way if I'd wanted, but I paused too long and I didn't die all the way. I know I should be happy. Happy to be with my dad, sleep in my room, cuddle with my dog, but I'm not. I don't feel solid enough to truly think it through even. Like there's water between my atoms.

I get a little better everyday. The nightmares get fewer. The ones where I wake up screaming but no one can hear my scream because it's a silent underwater scream. Even here. Even above ground. The worst kind of scream. The dream gets shorter and shorter until it fades completely.

Fourth grade flies by. I start talking again just before school ends. The house was so quiet for so long. I never realized how little my dad spoke, not just how few the words are, but how little his voice is, until mine was gone also. Many nights you wouldn't know if someone was home at our house. Other nights it was just the droning on and on of the television.

I feel like a normal girl again and start doing normal girl things. I go to Bridget's house a lot. We have sleepovers. We talk about boys. But deep inside of me I am still drowning all the time. I'm mostly better, but something is broken and I can't find it and I feel like I never will. I run harder at things. I jump farther, climb higher. I do not look where I'm going, I do not care. My climbing tree is no longer my confidant, it challenges me, beckoning to see how high I can go, how far out I can climb on spindly branches, how long I'll stay as I dangle from them and they creak and bend and break.

■■■

Seventh grade. It's been three years since I drowned and, despite the constant sound of waves in my head, I mostly don't think about it. This is because there are new distractions.

At the beginning of the year we go to our lockers and unload the never-ending supplies our parents bought for us over the summer (or the day before in my dad's case). It's still too hot, summer is hanging on hard, and it's a chore to be in school, let alone carry a huge book bag through the halls. My body feels disjointed, like a wooden doll I used to have whose knees and elbows we interlocking joints that moved up and down, though everything else remained stationary.

Dad says it's part of growing up and that soon I'll be as tall as I'll ever be. But I wonder if he's right. Each day it feels like I get taller and I wonder if maybe I'm actually a tree with endless potential for growth.

My locker actually feels smaller to me than my elementary one despite being taller and wider. I'm so tall I dwarf it. I wonder if I'll fit in the desks.

I try and shake off how giraffe-like I feel and start putting my supplies in my locker. I know Tim and Steve will be next to me, as they always are, as they've been since kindergarten because your whole order in life is determined by your last name. What an odd way to decide who goes first and who last. Who will spend and entire lifetime sitting net to each other, observing daily rituals, and whom you'll nearly never see simply because your last name is Adams and theirs is Zeeger.

I guess it would be ok if Tim or Steve were of any interest to me, but they're all football and sweat and farm-boy language. They're fine, just different than me.

Steve shows up and puts his things away, chomping on a turkey sandwich, getting half in his mouth. He doesn't care if I see this. He may not even know I'm there. Tim does not show up. Tim is another locker down, meaning his locker is now open. I secretly hope for a girl like me. I don't actually know if there are any other girls like me, but I hope for one anyway on the off chance someone is listening. A girl who can play the part of a normal girl, but is anything but. A girl with corners. A girl with shadows where dreams go.

And for a second I think I'm getting my wish. Auburn hair is floating towards me, pretty features underneath. But when my eyes adjust I realize this is a boy. A boy with eyelashes framing his eyes. They look like centipede legs, terrifying and endlessly fascinating. I could watch them float up and down forever.

And then he's next to me and we're sharing the same air and I'm suddenly sick and happy. I give up trying to act cool. I put my books down. I turn to him. But before I can ask, as the words form in my throat, he shoots out his hand and tells me his name. It's a name I'll spend a lot of time caressing in my mind. It will solidify itself and almost become its own being. I'll draw it, over and over, until my hand is too sore and cramped to continue. I'll sing it and sigh it and get angry that I'll never say it perfectly because only he can do that, but he rarely says his own name. That's the greatest problem with naming humans. We rarely say our own name. Our identities instead are left in the mouths of others who often don't know how to say us at all.

I mumble my name and know it doesn't matter what my name is because I will answer to anything he says. Somehow, we both know. From that point on, we are one.

We spend a lot of time together. I know there are adult things we're supposed to be doing, but holding hands seems like the most dangerous thing on earth. That danger is addicting. He is my new tree and the branches seem much higher and thinner. We go to our first school dance together. Dad took me to the mall. I got a corduroy burgundy skirt, cream tights and a forest green shirt.

Some part of me knows dad should be talking to me about this. And that part of me is angry at him for not, but I don't know why. Sometimes he'll open his mouth and it's clear he wants to say something, but then he breathes in deeply and it's gone. It's like watching fog recede on spring mornings. From far away it looks solid, but once you try and prove its existence, it's gone—if it was ever really there at all.

In the summers we all run together on the beach, Maggie nipping at our heels. I swim still, just as far, just as deep because it's only in the water, under the water, I feel truly at home. Maggie watches from the sand. She has not forgotten. She will not relax.

She likes him. He stokes her ears and holds her. Throws sticks for her to chase. Talks to her in low tones and looks her in the eyes. She covers him in sloppy kisses.

Eighth grade comes and goes and I barely even register it.

Before I know it, I'm walking towards high school. I'm not scared because nothing is scary when you carry this much love in your heart. I'm not like my friends.

The last week of middle school I sat with my girlfriends in the early summer sun, saying goodbye to the playground in front of us. Some of them are wearing make-up. I started too, but Maggie chewed most of it up, and I never replaced it. Stacey Tamber was talking about who would be popular in high school. She said you could tell by who curled their bangs under and who curled them up. I never had bangs, or a mom to take me to a salon, so I wasn't too worried about it. I continued to feel how I always felt. Safely inside, but mostly invisible. And I liked it that way. I didn't want to feel solid. I like feeling like a liquid or a gas, able to disappear or spread out, dilute myself, not be seen. Fill any container, take its shape. How I'd always been.

They thought they all sounded so smart. Trying to sound so adult, when I was the only one doing adult things. I was the only one who'd seen a boy naked. I was the only one who'd been naked with a boy. I didn't talk about these things because they were delicious secrets that didn't seem to be anyone else's business. They were mine to hold. It was the only time I'd let myself take solid shape.

We'd also had sex ed that year. All of us had our periods now took care of them with the proper amount of repulsion and shame. Once a month some poor girl wore a white dress or thin pants and was humiliated by her own body. Since I didn't plan on ever having children the whole thing seemed like such a nuisance to me. I hadn't even told my dad. I just took my allowance to the store, read the inserts in the cardboard packages and figured it out. I'd taken over my own parenting by then. I'd become my own mother.

Our town was very, very religious and so a lot of the girl's parents wrote notes saying they could skip sex ed. I thought denying biology was dumb. My dad stayed mute on the subject. The class was mostly just explaining anatomy. None of how it worked. At the end we were given a condom. The boys blew theirs up into water balloons. Most boys are idiots. I'm lucky to have found the one that isn't. I wonder if my mom thought my dad was an idiot. She must have thought he wasn't if she decided to marry him, but who knows. A lot of my friend's parents got divorced since elementary school. Some of them are dating. It's gross and weird and my friends seem sad. Maybe I actually got off easy.

The class featured a working model of the uterus. While I'm not interested in what it produces, I did think it was very beautiful. One side perfectly reflecting the other, mirror images. The tubes like rivers leading to a lake. Coming together to make something bigger than themselves. But then the boys got ahold of the little plastic ovaries and started throwing them to each other. Again, boys are dumb.

But not my boy. My boy is sweet and smart and his gender is secondary to who he is. I think no matter how he'd been made, I still would have loved him. And he'd feel the same about me. My need to be with him, sharing his air, smelling his skin is so strong sometimes I feel completely insane. I have no girlfriends anymore because I have no need for anyone else.   We're inseparable. Like twins. A lot of girls are already talking about marriage, but that's not this kind of love. Marriage is irrelevant. We need no one else involved in this. Sometimes I wonder what my mom would have thought of all this. Would I have her support? Would she have been more strict than my dad? I don't know.

For someone who's been largely quiet on the subject of my life, dad suddenly has some opinions. And most of those opinions are that mine are irrelevant. I don't know what he's scared of. He talks at me—I could be anyone, any young girl in his charge. He has no clue who I am. I doubt he could identify me in a line-up. It's like he's working off a script from a movie he thinks we're in. He says the lines, presses forward without listening to the other character. As though his job is done simply through speaking.

He does not hear me.

I'm not sure he ever has.

I wonder how much different life would be if my mom was here, though in a lot of ways I think it would be much the same. But maybe she would understand when I tell her I'm sick with love. It's hard to describe to someone who maybe never has had that kind of love in their lives. Whom you're not sure even truly exists. But maybe my mom was a ghost person too. Maybe my parents were ghost people passing through each other and leaving me as the physical outcome.

I start sneaking out. A lot of girls I know do it. I'm not the only one. Tenth grade is full of girls disobeying orders and I'm just one in a line of hormonal AWOL soldiers. I need to see him. I have to see him. He's the beach and I'm the water and we do not exist without each other.

I open the window and start to silently maneuver my body through it. It's early spring and the cool lake air washes over my perpetually warm body. I'm warm all the time now. Except my hands. My hands have never been warm since the day in the lake. He has a car and he waits by the road. He knows I'm coming. I can already smell him, taste his lips on mine. I'm wearing the lipstick he likes. I like leaving my mark on him. Hot pink smudges like fingerprints at the scene of the crime. You are mine, they say. I am yours.

Then a pull on the hem of my jeans. It's small, a slight tug. I try to move through the window but it's like I'm caught on something I can't see in the darkness of my room. I pull free and the room fills with a loud howl, then a raucous bark. It's Maggie. I try and shush her—she's been such a pain in the ass lately—but she will not be quiet. I could murder her. I imagine tossing her through the window. My heart breaks into a thousand pieces. She has stolen from me. I feel a great emptiness inside. Like I'm thirsty and all there is is seawater. It isn't long before my dad is in my room. Maggie jumps on the bed and looks me in the eye. Then she contentedly curls up on my pillow and falls fast asleep.

I will never forgive her for this. I think almost nothing weeks later as I tell dad I can no longer take care of her.

I take my life back. I leave the window cracked at all times.

Everything is good. Everything is right. If there is a storm coming I do not see it.

CHAPTER 9

I'm being born again, but it's so slow I barely realize it. Something cracks open. Something shoots up and something shoots down. I am so thirsty. And hungry too, but not for anything I've been hungry for before. I reach hard, both up and down, trying to stretch myself as big as I can. Trying to reach the water below me and the sun above me. Trying to warm up and cool down at the same time.

I am struck once again by how hard it is to be born. You are one of so many choices; so many others are thrown away, discarded, fertilizer for the next batch. But you, you are here. Against all odds every time, you are here.

Days pass and I become, slowly, a mirror image of myself. As I reach up and out I equally reach down and through. I am a stagnant, still image of lightening both above and below the earth. Above I am rife with life, below I appear unremarkable. As I reach down and away, securing myself, reaching for water, seeking soil nutrients, I am connected to all that has been. I am living history and I know all of the stories that have been told. I am recycled from the past and yet a new thing now—a conglomerate of all that fell here before me or was washed here by the waters underground.

But I am not just any tree. I am her tree. I am my own tree.

I cannot hear or see or taste. But I can vibrate and I can feel vibrations. I know a bird from a chipmunk. I know a robin from a crow. I know the male from a female and I know if they are relaxed or hungry, full or nervous. I can feel a woodpecker drill into my bones and it feels good to be so necessary and useful and to have the insects plucked from my bark.

I know when there's an earthquake in India long before it happens. I know when drought is coming. I know when the snow falls heavy and wet. I know what other roots my roots touch and we communicate through the soil. Messages sent by slugs and termites. Knotty appendages holding hands. We fight to survive while living in harmony. We agree that some must die and on the reasons why and there is no sadness or remorse, just a deep understanding that it will be better for all. I hear the voices of all things echoed through the sediment, a messaging system that never stops, never sleeps, though slows down when the ground freezes and things must pause.

I don't know how long I'm here. I have no verbiage for keeping track of the amount of springs and summers that come and go. I am myself, yes, but I am also this tree and I am somewhat limited by the needs of being a tree.

I know this tree. I understand now that I have always known this tree and that there is a reason I spent all my years as a child wrapped in its arms, mothered by it, loved by it. And that my daughter has felt the same pull, the same draw, the same need and desire to be at its tips and limbs, to feel more free than possible on the ground and not know why.

The first few years (is it 5 or 50? I don't know) are a daily struggle. I reach for the sun, doing my best to fulfill my destiny without knowing it. I know my only job is to try my best to survive. Some part of me knows that I will because I've already met myself in the future, already joined my soul with its missing pieces.

I am not terribly strong and don't seem fated to live long. I serve my purpose, big in its own way, but I can't see how I will become what I know to be true. Then it happens.

The soil beneath me loosens and I find myself increasing my grip just to stay where I am. I no longer am fighting for sun or food or nitrogen. I no longer need move my roots carefully along the web of other roots. I instinctively burst forward, spread out, take the real estate that's been offered me.

Then I realize what's happened.

I am alone, or nearly alone. The huge forest that was my home is now gone. There is only me. Their death allowed my life.

Because I am alone and strong I become home to so many living creatures. And of course, myself and later, my daughter. Seasons, years, come and go. I feel tidal waves and earthquakes. A volcano explodes. Other things too. I feel the earth changing, dying, poisoned. It doesn't feel cursed or doomed though. Just a death, like so many other deaths. A pathway to the next thing.

I wait for her. I will know her weight, feel the vibration of her laughter. I will hold her in my arms and keep her safe and alive. I will be to her what I could not. I will be patient.

I weather droughts and floods. Deep freezes and scorching summers. Infestations and viruses. But still I stand, waiting.

This is a different waiting. I am not filled with panic or a need to find her immediately. I know she is still just a mix of carbon and oxygen that is a part of some many other things—split between water and soil and plant and bird. She is not whole yet, but existing in other things. She is not here, but she has always been here. I will know when she has arrived. When I have helped her arrive. I know that I will also be in two places at once. That I will exist here, but also not here. My soul split in two, weaker than it should be. I see now why that was. I see now why I never felt whole. Why I was not connected to myself, to this world, but tenuously, by only a thread.

Time runs its course and I am strong now. Giant and strong, a tower marking the landscape. I feel the sun fully on my arms, in my bones. I convert it to energy. But I feel something new too. I am no longer alone. Thousands of smaller brothers and sisters, vying for the same nutrients I have maintained solo custody of. I am happy to feel them. I am happy the birds will find new homes. The squirrels will find new food sources.

I will not need things much longer anyway. I am cracking on the inside. My roots still reach and push, but they are slower now, less relentless in their pursuit. I am drying out, no longer able to pump water to every place that needs it. Whole areas of my immense compound have been walled off and abandoned, left to die and decay, to protect what little new growth each season brings. I am happy to meet my replacements. I will be happy to feed them when I fall—to make room for the next generation.

I am here. By which I mean, both of us are here. I feel my other half near by. I feel the acorn in my stomach. It plants roots, reaching and stretching, finding the nutrients I have to offer it. I feel her there. My energy soars just being near her presence. After all this time, all these travels, all these lives, I will finally be whole again, if only for a moment. Luckily time is mine to bend, and I can make that moment last forever.

In a sea of years the next few go by like minutes. I'm sure I shed and grow, reach and sleep, but I barely notice it. Then one day something heavy hangs on my lowest branches. Too big to be a squirrel or raccoon.

It's her. She's here. I stretch a little wider to give her room. To welcome her. Her giggles form sound waves that travel through my tough skin and into the places most quiet inside of me. They fill in the gaps. They make a part a whole. I know what I will be to her. I know we are intertwined, forever a part of each other. I feel no pain or fear or panic anymore. I feel peace.

I feel her hands too small still to fully encircle even my lowest rungs.

But I know they will grow. I know we will learn together. How to be there for each other. How I will be there to solace, to comfort, to encourage, to protect. To provide both safety and an exhilarating place to take risks. How I will help her see her own strength and learn her own limitations.

To mother.

Years go by and hands get bigger. She climbs higher and higher, daring to hang near the offshoots I know are not strong enough to hold her.

On occasion, she cries. The water streams down my leaves and is absorbed and for brief seconds our beings wholly mix. I feel her. I know her story. But more often than tears there is laughter. Raucous, full-bellied laughter. Even as she gets bigger, so does the vibration of happiness her body makes when she is with me.

I am here for her.

I am here for her in so many ways. At times fragmented from myself. I am a mosquito. I am a bird. I am a dog. I am all these things in turn and yet always here. Each one learning more about her. More about me.

There are other energies that join her. One I get to know quite well. He comes with her, climbs with her, together, up and up. He does not hold her back. The laughter increases, its frequency lower and deeper than it has been. She's grown. Not fully, her bones have not yet set with the density and hardness of adulthood, but here she is, mostly formed. With his help she gets higher than she has been, tries harder to reach the top, feels supported and free. Like any risk she takes will be rewarded.

Some days I feel them nestled together near the ground, backs against me for support. Together they create a warmth I feel deep down to my core. It's always August between them—hot and sweet, memories of the long summer past, an eye to the future.

And then it's winter again and she is alone. Once, twice...the pattern has changed. She chooses the lowest most rung. Dares to climb no more. Reaches no higher.

Something about her has changed.

For the first time I curse my lack of eyes, lack of voice. I need to talk to her, to see her, for her to see me. It's nearing time for me to move on again and I can feel it. My roots are curling into themselves, no longer seeking out water. The areas of my body I've left to decay have grown large and brittle. I cannot leave now. She needs me.

One day she starts to climb. Tentatively at first, but gradually gaining ferocity. Like nothing could keep her from the top. She passes the places she's stopped in the past. Reaching up, up, up. Her sweat drips on me. It feels of fear and sadness and something I cannot place.

She is so high now and I know she will fall. I cannot support her weight on my spindly most parts. I feel something glide over my limbs.

And I know now. I know what must be done.

I let go. I let go from my deepest most crevices. And like a house of sticks I begin to crack. Gaining momentum as weight pushes on weight.

As I separate from myself. As time stands still. And I am released.

CHAPTER 10

I like to wear my pants real low on my hips. I like how the skin there stretches like a canvas over a wood frame. I like how when I raise my hand my shirt rides up just enough to feel the way the school air conditioner forces air over my skin. I like how he watches for that patch to appear, then pretends to listen to my answer.

I remember not wanting to grow up, thinking adults were terrible.

Now they're all I can think about. I've joined them and I feel their call thrumming away on my insides, pulsating with the rest of humanity. I try not to think too much about anything, because that's when I lose that intoxicating feeling. Thinking removes me from them. Puts me outside.

I don't like being outside.

I like school because I am bored by it in the most delightful way. I'm bored by the people, the conversations—but the future we all share, so shiny and filled with intentions—it's worth showing up for. And, of course, there's him.

I don't like being home. I'm outside even when I'm inside. Dad's there but in the same way he's always been gone. We both eat dinner with the TV on just so someone is having a conversation. I don't like to think about it because then I feel the dark water threatening to come up, regurgitating in my throat, bringing the past and her questions with it. Not thinking too much is the answer at home too.

Mr. Denson is too young to be a teacher. He's only 24. In the real world we'd date openly. Maybe he'd take me to prom. We've already decided I'll go alone to prom so that we can pretend we're there together even though we can't touch or dance or talk. We'll do all those things later. In the dark. In his car. Parked by the beach. At the end of the year when I graduate we'll get married maybe. Or he'll move so I can go to college out of state. Or whatever. The future is full of intentions. And all the turns seem right.

I liked science even before he became my teacher. I'm still considering biology. The study of life. That always makes me laugh. How can you study something as unpredictable as life? Maybe I'd be better off in mortuary science. Death is something I know a lot about. My mom. My bird. My dog. James.

James.

After he died I didn't think I'd ever want to kiss anyone again. I watched him die. At 15 I stood in his hospital room. They said he was brain dead already. He hadn't been wearing a helmet. His bike now just pieces that could fit in your pocket. He'd been on his way to see me. And now he was dead. He was going to be a writer. He was going to write me, he said, in the same way a painter paints his muse. He'd write me as a book, as a poem—he'd use his words to sculpt me into something that would live forever, never age, be solidified in the universe. But now his brain was trapped and his fingers mute.

Still so beautiful.

I held his hand, laced his fingers through mine and smelled his hair. It smelled of boy. Summer and dirt and sweat and the beginning surges of testosterone flooded my nose. I kissed his cheek. There was gravel imbedded in it. I tried to say goodbye but I was so tired of saying goodbye. So I just sat there. I did not cry. I do not cry. I stopped thinking all together. There seems to be no use in it.

Whatever of me had begun to die in the lake that day as a kid; it died completely when I let go of his hand.

Starting school the next year was like moving under water. I saw and knew everything and everyone, but all the edges seemed soft. All the features eroded and blurred.

But then he popped into focus.

I hadn't even chosen AP Science. I didn't really care where I was supposed to be, but also didn't care enough to not be there. I went where I was told. Did what I was supposed to do. On the weekends my friends and I sat around on dunes, smoking joints and drinking cheap strawberry flavored wine. We are so loud, but we're saying nothing. Just filling up empty space. Seeing how big we can be before we carve ourselves down to fit into an office chair, or station wagon or someone else's idea of us.

I'm somewhere between the burnouts and the popular kids. The thing is; I'm beautiful. I do not care about this. But, I can also see that beauty gives you a currency to belong anywhere at anytime. I also recognize its danger. People can hate for something you are not doing, for a person you are not. I do not even look at mirrors because the emptiness in my own eyes scares me. The way my dad jumps when I enter a room scares me. The way I am not safe in parking lots, grocery stores, beaches…scares me. I'm not sure how anyone else focuses on me as a solid object when I feel stretched so thin, the space between my pieces so far apart.

Then he looks at me.

It's the first day of class and I take my assigned seat in the first row. He's at his desk. He looks like no one I've ever seen. His hair floats around him, moving in directions it seems to have created for itself. Tight curls moving against gravity and with gravity. It's nearly impossible to see it and not want to stick your finger deep into a curl and marvel at how it disappears. To not want to pull on one and watch it spring back. They carry the sun in them. Hours logged outside, stealing the color from sections, leaving it in others; like the patchy shade in the woods, creating a pattern, but not the key to the pattern. His arms hold more clues. Bare and ropey they are smattered with tan freckles so thick it's not clear that they aren't the original owners of this real estate.

I'm studying these things when he looks up. And it's over before it starts. Like watching a play in reverse. We already know the ending.

I'm not scared and I don't think about it. I tell my dad I'm out with friends. I tell the friends my dad won't let me leave. I almost laugh when I say it; the thought of my dad caring either way is so unbelievable. But their dads are normal and they ask no questions.

There's one night where I am lying and my dad looks at me. He actually looks at me. In my eyes. He sees me. I almost breakdown and tell him the truth because the feeling of my dad seeing me is so overwhelmingly odd. For a moment he just listens. Then he says, "You look so much like your mother." He immediately turns around and goes back to doing the dishes or folding laundry or whatever else it is that he does to continue existing until he dies. In a lot of ways I think he's already decided he's passed on. A corporeal ghost. A soul robot. I try sometimes to look back and see where I lost him, but mostly I think I never had him to begin with. He died with my mom. I was born an orphan with a living parent. I think it happens all the time.

I used to think I'd never have kids because who in the hell wants to do this to someone? Particularly someone you love? But now I'm not so sure because what if? What if it could be different? What if I could right the wrongs? What if, simply by not dying, I could have a real family? It's a new dream, and I indulge it more often than I should.

The windows of the car are steamed up so thick the outside world isn't even there anymore. We shut the heat off a long time ago. He stops. He's worried we'll be found out. That my dad will kill him. That he'll get fired. He never intended this to happen, he says.

For a moment I'm so taken aback at the thought my dad would care at all that I miss the rest of what he's saying. It never occurred to me that he could go to jail. And I don't want to hear any of this. I can't hear anything anyway over the hum of my body, the blood rushing in my ears, the deafening feeling of the salty sweat that covers my bare skin, begging to be toughed. My brain is too far-gone for thought. I open my mouth and lay it over his. He is quiet now. This is good.

Spring is coming. I feel it pushing through the earth, violent and beautiful. Such brutal force to shoot up the most delicate things. I'm happy to be out of school soon. I got a summer job selling ice cream at the beach. It sounds easy and thoughtless and I'm happy to have a job I can bike to everyday. I got a bike freshman year that I bought for myself with birthday money. I'd always wanted a bike. That never changed. Even when all the other kids my age were saving up for a car or counting the days until drivers training, I only wanted to bike. I'd rather not just be sitting. My brain gets too busy then. I'd rather be hurling myself down the street, barely staying upright, ground a blur beneath my Converse.

But also, I feel different. I feel off. Somewhere beneath the placid happiness of teenagerhood there is something not right. It's like when the lake is calm on the surface but beneath it angry currents from Wisconsin are headed your way, to suck you under, bury you in black.

I get hit with the stomach flu the first week of April.

And again, the second week.

And again the third.

I'm not dumb. I'm studying biology. I get it. I know what's up. I'm not even the first one at my school to have this happen. I'm even, maybe, hopeful.

But then, he just stops talking to me. He pretends that I do not exist. He actually gives me a demerit when I touch his arm. He sends me to the principal's office. The principle informs me that I have an unhealthy obsession with my teacher and I'll be moving classrooms. He tells me not to worry. He tells me I'm not the first young lady to become obsessed with this teacher.

I realize I probably am not. I'm probably not the first at all.

How do you tell an apparition you're pregnant? How do you talk to the dead of the living? I try to tell my dad but I can't breathe and I'm drowning in words of vague intention.

Once again there is something uninvited inside of me, dictating life, taking it from me.

The next month I see the world the way I think my father does. All manner of grey ideas of objects are before me. I speak when spoken to, but I am not sure it is the right language. I live outside of myself and everyone around me is so caught up in themselves they do not notice.

I need to think. I need to find a way to make sense of what this life has been. There is a part of me still fighting to breathe. Still making a run at the future. But the larger part of me screams that I'm not even supposed to be here. That I somehow slipped through the cosmic womb despite her best efforts to keep me safe and warm. That I released myself into this cold and dark world with two ghost parents.

I go where I always go to think. I go to the tree. I imagine I've always gone there and always will go there, no matter the time or manner.

I avoided her for so long.

I climb the first branch, feeling the strength of my arms, the dexterity of my fingers. I marvel at how good it feels. How this is the closest I've ever been to myself. I feel more alive than I have in years. I pull and pull until I reach my normal resting place. I pause, but the ground looks too close. I'm too close to where my problems live and it propels me higher until I'm dizzy from the climb and my waning breath. From where I am I can see now across the dune. I see the lake. The smokestack out in Gary, Indiana, throwing its haze out into a pink and orange sunset. I smell the rain coming in. The familiar scent of the dark black dirt resting just below the dune's sandy face, mixing with the lake water being carried by the air in an invisible dance that will end where it began. I think of how many times this has all happened without me or any other human to ponder it, to watch it, to judge it.

I pull faster now and I'm nearing the top. A small branch breaks below me and for a moment I teeter there, suspended in air, held up by god knows what. And for a minute I'm floating in the air and I remark at how like floating in the water it is. My feet catch a limb and I catch my breath. I look out at the dim light across the dune. I try and remember why I'm here. I cannot remember. I take one last look around. I plant my feet. I bend my knees. I'm ready to finish what the lake started. I'm ready to return. And just as I'm about to jump there's a terrifying snap somewhere deep within the tree. Branches are throwing themselves side to side. Instinct forces me to grab on to the thickest branch before it sideswipes me. And before I know it, I'm safely on the ground, the tree gently planting me on the earth.

I turn around and look at the destruction behind me. The tree is completely in half, spilt perfectly down the middle. Like it had always been two parts that became a whole temporarily. I plant myself in its center and hope that I grow where it once was.

CHAPTER 11

I'm being born again, but this time I remember it from the first time. I wiggle my toes, admiring their dexterity. I take a moment to clasp my hands together and open my eyes. I'm still in that place none of us should see. That place between being and not being; where who we are is combined with what we are. I know this is the last time I'll see it. And I am glad for that.

The next time I see anything close to it will be in the eyes of the little girl I'll hold in my arms. And my tongue will not pause as I say her name.

Thank you to: Andy Carey, Karisa Bruin (for being willing to chase down crazy ideas with me), Sunny Wood, Jack Lessenberry, Kelly Leonard, Cara Trautman (for so many great summers on the shore), Amber Britton (for 20-plus years of friendship), my mom (for encouraging my love of the outdoors), Liz Thompson, anyone who fights to protect Lake Michigan and its unrivaled shoreline and my son; for allowing me the gift of being his mother.